COLLEGE OF MARIN LIBRARY
KENTFIELD, CALIFORNIA

LOVING BELLE STARR

BRIGHT LEAF SHORT FICTION II

LOVING BELLE STARR

ROBERT TAYLOR, JR.

ALGONQUIN BOOKS
Chapel Hill

Acknowledgment is gratefully made to the editors of the publications mentioned below.

"Pearl Starr Alive in Arizona" was first published in *Obras*. "The Fiddler" was first published in *The Agni Review* under the title, "Loving Belle Starr." "Jim Reed" was first published in *Bachy* under the title, "The Hands of Jesse James." "Eddy the Boy" was first published under the title, "Hideout, Younger's Bend, c. 1874," and is reprinted with permission of *The North American Review*, ©1981 by the University of Northern Iowa. "Sam Starr" was first published in *Center* under the title, "Legends." "Jim July Starr" was first published in *Northwest Review* under the title, "Grim Want and Misery." "Eddy the Man" was first published under the title, "The Spirit of Belle Starr," in *The California Quarterly*, ©1982 by the Regents of the University of California. "The Death of Belle Starr" was first published in *Magazine*. "Mrs. Jesse James, Mourning" was first published in *Ontario Review* under the title, "Mourning." "The History of Frank James" was first published in the *Cimarron Review* and is reprinted here with the permission of the Board of Regents for Oklahoma State University, holders of the copyright, ©1981. "The Liberation of the Youngers" was first published in *Berkeley Monthly*. "Quantrill" was first published in the *Cimarron Review* and is reprinted here with the permission of the Board of Regents for Oklahoma State University, holders of the copyright, ©1981. "The Liberation of the Youngers" was first published in the *Cimarron Review* and is reprinted here with the permission of the Board of Regents for Oklahoma State University, holders of the copyright, ©1980. "Zerelda James Samuel" was first published in *The Agni Review* under the title, "Passing Away." "Charley Ford Betrayed" was first published in *Quarry West* under the title, "Jesse James Betrayed." "Billy Gashade and Glory" was first published in *The Georgia Review* under the title, "The James Boys Ride Again." "The Tragedy of Bob Ford" was first published in the *Cimarron Review* under the title, "The Tragedy of Jesse James," and is reprinted here with the permission of the Board of Regents for Oklahoma State University, holders of the copyright, ©1982. "Glory" was first published in *Prairie Schooner* under the title, "Presences."

The author would also like to express his appreciation to the librarians of the Oklahoma Historical Society in Oklahoma City, the Missouri Historical Society in St. Louis, the Western History Collection of the University of Oklahoma Library, and the Bertrand Library of Bucknell University.

Algonquin Books
P.O. Box 2225, Chapel Hill, NC 27515-2225

© 1984 by Robert Taylor, Jr.

Printed in the United States of America

All rights reserved. Except for brief quotation in critical articles or reviews, this book, or parts thereof, must not be reproduced in any form without permission in writing from the publisher. For further information contact Algonquin Books.

ISBN 0-912697-07-5

Library of Congress Cataloging in Publication data will be found on the last page of this book.

Illustrations used in the book are by Patricia Grossman.

CONTENTS

I LOVING BELLE STARR

Pearl Starr Alive in Arizona   3
The Fiddler   16
Jim Reed   27
Eddy the Boy   37
Sam Starr   49
Jim July Starr   61
Eddy the Man   73
The Death of Belle Starr   85

II FINDING JESSE JAMES

Quantrill   101
Mrs. Jesse James, Mourning   113
The History of Frank James   124
The Liberation of the Youngers   137
Charley Ford Betrayed   149
Billy Gashade and Glory   164
Glory   177
The Tragedy of Bob Ford   189
Zerelda James Samuel   203

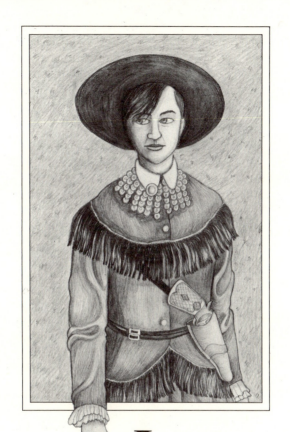

I
LOVING BELLE STARR

PEARL STARR ALIVE IN ARIZONA

The Bandit Queen's Daughter in the Flesh

She was a little drunk maybe, and not thinking as straight as she might usually, but she supposed she knew a thing or two. Hang around. Could she get you something, a glass of whisky, a beer, a little snack. She smiles, and you see that at one time it must have been a damn fine smile, enough devil in it to give any man pause, and she adjusts herself, a small pallid woman with rouged cheeks and tightly curled pitch black hair, in the overstuffed chair, crossing her legs the way a man does, one foot propped on her frail knee, and she unscrews the lid on the bottle of good rye whisky you've brought her and takes a fair swallow, her eyes opening wide. Have a swig, she says. You need to be thinking clearly, but don't want to make her feel uncomfortable and so accept the bottle. That's the way, she says. Now what was it you was wanting to know about.

Who Killed Belle Starr

She remembers. It was a long time ago, but you don't forget. She remembers Milo Hoyt, Frog they used to call him, come running up to the cabin shouting something fierce. She's alone, is Pearl, thinking about her baby over there in Siloam Springs, Arkansas, with Grandma Reed, her pink and pretty little Flossie the spitting image of her daddy. It's a wonder nobody but her can see it, but a good thing too, considering what *her* mama—that's the Bandit Queen she's talking about, you know—might do was she to know the identity of the man whose spent seed made Flossie. It wasn't going to kill her not to know. None of her damn business.

You sure you don't want a glass. You don't mind drinking from the bottle after me? Bless your heart, honey—it's sweet of you to say it.

So I'm sitting there by the fire, for it was cold, February you know, thinking about little Flossie, when I hear the shouting outside, then the pounding on the door and Frog Hoyt jumping in, his face red as a beet, his breath coming heavy, and a smell —Lord, how that man did smell, a little like a sweat-slick horse, a little like green wood burning. He was a small man, was Frog Hoyt, with a wide mouth and little round eyes.

Your mama's killed, he says.

And that was that. That is how I come to find out.

Watson

Watson, she says. We never knew where he came from, who exactly he was. He was just there one day, with a wife that looked like a piece of beefsteak done up in ribbons, and a brand new wagon so shiny and clean you'd think its wheels never set foot on dirt before that moment. He had a way of looking at you, grinning like he knew you, all right, sure, had just been thinking about you and seeing you in his head the minute you appeared before him in the flesh. He had managed to get a tract of land next to our own. We didn't know how. It wasn't no Cherokee bride he had riding with him up in that wagon. Maybe he had some blood in him, we never knew, but he looked white through and through. This would have been '86, I believe, '87 the very latest, since Mama passed away in '89, and in them days they was plenty of low-lifers and wastrels coming into the Territory, crossing on the old California Road that runs just south of the river, skimpy horses pulling them old Weber wagons piled high with Lord knows what paraphernalia, trunks and crates held together with nothing more than butcher twine and covered with dust, and children flimsy-looking as the other baggage. These folks was all sniffing for land, you see, drifting east from the Strip, then back through it, then escorted out of the Territory by the Buffalo Soldiers. Oh, that land had to be opened up. It was just a question of when, and when that time came they was going to be there, on the spot, ready to stake a claim come hell or high water. Them Indians—and they meant the Cheyennes and the Arapahoes and the Kiowas and Comanches and the like, the ones west of the crosstimbers that still lived in their hide lodges and hunted for buffalo long gone and that had to depend, therefore, on the government to ration them out beef and beans; they didn't mean *our* Indians, the Cherokee and Choctaw and the like that was farming and trading and getting religion and learning and doing just fine, thank you—them wild Indians, you see, did not *deserve* the land that was give to them. They did not take advantage of it, and so it rightfully belonged to them that would. It was justice. And the government was bound to see the truth, just like everybody else had already seen it for years. They was right. If you have read your history book, why, you know they was right. The first lands was opened up in '89, year Mama passed on.

But Watson, *he* stopped. In '86, I believe it was, or '87, and he had the land already deeded to him, good bottom land just acrost the river in the Choctaw nation alongside our own. He had that shiny wagon and big dark horses with ripply hocks and broad flanks and teeth like knives, and when we rode out to see what become of him—this not two weeks after he tipped his hat and grinned at us from his wagonseat—he had a two-room house with a dog-run, already standing, a shed building nearby, a field in dark long furrows stretching out behind the house so perfect you'd think it was just a big picture of a field laid down there on top of what would be rank weeds and scrub oaks, a field such as would be found nowhere save in the minds of Boomers and such like fools who see only what they want to see. But there it was, and Watson was the one that had it.

Comment on Her Brother Eddy

She never understood him, he wanted something, it seemed like, that he wasn't never going to get, not just the killing of Watson, something else. She never could find out what. She remembers how he used to like to hear their mama read to them. Oh, yes, she was a educated woman. She had books. I wish to goodness I knew all she did. Maybe she even understood her Eddy, I don't know. She cared for him more than she cared for me, though that's not saying much because she didn't take to me a-tall. I was her duty, he was her joy. And he worshipped her in return. Maybe all he wanted was to sit at her feet all day and listen to her read him poems or play him songs on the piano. Oh, yes, she had a piano. A big one. A St. Louis piano, she always said it was a St. Louis piano. I don't know whatever become of that piano.

Eddy died looking for Watson. This would be in '96. He believed Watson done it, and meant to track him down. Judge Parker made Eddy a marshal. Watson hadn't been seen since the hearing. They had found his shotgun near the place Mama was shot, but that wasn't enough evidence. Eddy went near crazy trying to find Watson. Some say Judge Parker made Eddy a marshal so as to get him shot. It was a good bet in them days.

Eddy was killed in a saloon in Wagoner, I.T. They never found nobody to arrest.

Who Belle Starr Loved

No one. In Pearl's opinion. I never met Cole Younger, Pearl says. If he was my father, why, he never cared to admit it. Jim Reed was the father of Eddy. Dead, they're all dead now. Jim Reed and Sam Starr and Jim July and I don't know who all else, they're all dead, all her lovers, and she didn't love a one of them. No, there's no love between a man and woman. Grief's more like it. And Commerce. That's what she's learned from her mama.

They're all dead now. Only Baby Pearl is still alive. And that is because I have done without the grief and am my own woman.

She sits straight in the overstuffed chair, her head cocked to one side as if she hears something out the window. She holds onto the bottle of rye whisky but she hasn't drunk from it for some time now. You get the feeling that what she says surprises her and she wants to sit in silence a moment and think about what she has heard. The wind blows soft against the window panes and you can see that deep Arizona sky with its frail white clouds skittering on the surface of it like they come loose from some other sky.

Mama loved no one, she says, passing the bottle of whisky. For sure not me.

Flossie's Father

Watson? Hell, no. That man couldn't have fathered nothing. Why, that pretty field lay there furrowed and barren, nothing ever come up save more of what must have been there before he sunk his shiny new share into it, stinkweed and bunched bluestem, and that sparse and pitiful-looking. Oh, there was plenty of men in them days could've claimed her for a bride, had they a mind to and her mama's consent. Jim July? That was her mama's man. She remembers his long hair, dark and straight, hanging clear down to his shoulders. He was what you call a wiry man, but with sad eyes like a hound and smooth high cheekbones. A Creek Indian. His people settled up around where Tulsa is today, probably in the middle of one of them big oil fields on a tract that they was no doubt cheated out of in the time of the allotments. He was gone before it was.

She always had a liking for Jim July, him so quiet and bashful, but all he cared about was her mama, his loving Belle. Even called himself Starr, and when she was shot I do think he was a raving maniac the rest of his life, what there was left of it. Some thought *he* killed her, but what would he do a thing like that for. A young fellow named Hutchins believed it and chased Jim July Starr all over the Territory until he shot him and killed him. This was over somewhere in the old Chickasaw Nation, near Ardmore, and would have been in '90 or '91, not much more than a year after Mama's death. Jim July was a sweet, peaceful man. It was too bad for him he got in with the likes of Mama and me.

The father of Flossie, well, she's kept him a secret all these years and she reckons she'll say no more this close to the end. Put it down, she says, that I don't rightly remember.

How They Amused Themselves

It was easy. In them days it was fiddling and dancing. Whisky was plentiful, woods nearby and hills honeycombed with caves. A body could do most anything. The law was Fort Smith and the Lighthorsemen. Fort Smith was a long ways and the Lighthorsemen most always someplace else, chasing whisky-runners. We was free. Our own law. Even the old Cherokees feared us—because we was Starrs, you see, and therefore under the protection of the meanest Cherokee of them all, old Tom Starr. We had the dances, let me tell you. None of this radio music. The real thing: fiddles and banjos.

I remember my mama dancing. I had to sit and watch, listen to that fiddle music and feel my own blood stirring, my heart jumping for the desire to get out there and dance, but I wasn't allowed. I must watch until I was old enough. Mama could dance, and dance all night, did do it many a time, even the night her Sam Starr was shot by Frank West. Why do you think you to have stop, she asked that fiddler. A little yell now and then, that was what I had to content myself with. She was going to make me into a lady, her Pearl Younger, her Canadian Lily. And ladies didn't dance before their time.

Pearl smiled, sipped the whisky, licked her lips, looked me straight in the eye but as though seeing in me someone I never dreamed of being. I took the bottle when she handed it to me, that whisky tasting better and better, my blood warming to the woman sitting across from me, the Pearl Starr I'd dreamed of finding, knowing she had to be alive somewhere, the only one who would have survived, who *could* have survived those years. And here she was, alive in Arizona, her face not plump like in the old pictures, all the more stark from the red patted onto it, her thin lips, blue beneath the flaking red, scarce moving save when she prepared them to accept the mouth of the bottle. Then they quivered slightly and grew suddenly fuller and I imagined they looked that way when, years ago, she drew her arms around a lover and pulled him to her.

The Spiritual Life

Mainly it was a matter of the missions. We was raised up to believe like Christians believe, she says, same as most everybody else. Mama read to us from the Bible and taught us to sing Nearer My God to Thee and, later, we heard her bang out the hymns on the piano. A Mighty Fortress Is Our God. That was her favorite. I am a soprano, Mama used to tell us. Someone, she was always saying, once told her she should go into a conservatory and train herself to sing operas, but there was never the opportunity. Once in a while a preacher came through, rode up on a lanky horse that looked near death, hooves split and tail frazzled, no color to speak of, the preacher himself with small eyes and small white hands, that's what I remember, the small white hands laying flat on the tabletop until he took to talking, and a voice that sounded like it was more used to singing the words instead of saying them. I like to hear them talk. Afterwards Eddy and me'd go down by the river and Eddy'd stand up on the big rock and preach to me just like I was a crowd. He could remember every word that preacher said and I believe he'd a-made a good preacher had he lived long enough and give up that looking everywhere for Watson that was bound to get him in trouble.

The best missions was the Choctaw ones, Mama used to say, but we was not particular, seldom going in any of them. My Grandma Reed up in Missouri was a church-goer and used to take me along with her when I was staying with her. I liked it all right. I got to dress fancy and watch farm boys get hot under their stiff collars. They never paid much attention to the sermons, as any girl could see, and I never was much for them either, they wasn't a match for the missionaries that came to save us at Younger's Bend.

Some of the old Cherokees didn't go to the missions. They had old superstitions that their grandfathers taught them and they wasn't about to give them up. That's what the preacher told us. The Seminoles was the worst. They might dress like everybody else, but that was as far as it went. Beyond them, out there past the crosstimbers, amongst Cheyenne and Arapaho, there was no hope.

The Legends That Are Told

Everybody had a story about Belle Starr. How she rides up one day and says, Bill (or Harvey or Tom or Ben), have you a hunk of cornbread for a weary traveler, and leaves a couple of greenbacks where they don't find it for a day or two, stuck in a chink near the door or in the bottom of a mug in the pantry. She had been every place, it seems, and she knew everybody, and lived, to hear some say, years and years after she died. A fierce drinker, some said, that held her own with any peeler. A teetotaler, others said, never touched a drop in her life.

Pearl laughs, letting her foot drop to the floor.

Have you ever, I ask, heard the one about the fiddler?

There was always plenty of them around, she says. We all liked fiddle music, like I was saying.

This was about one that died while playing the fiddle for your mama. He was up at the caves, standing near the edge, and she was inside where it was cool, listening. Someone must not have liked that idea much. Some fellow, the story goes, followed the two of them out there, and when he looked up and saw that fiddler standing at the edge of the mouth of the cave stroking the strings of his fiddle, this fellow decided he had an opportunity too good to let pass by. He took aim and fired, and the fiddler fell. You never heard this story?

No, I never heard it at all.

The rest of it is this: When they looked for the body of that fiddler, they never could find it. And of course the fiddle was gone too.

Lordy.

And now they say if you go there near the cave, not just any time, the night of the Harvest Moon, and listen hard, why, you'll hear that fiddler playing just as sweet as ever, the music coming through the trees as sure as moonlight.

Ain't that a pretty story though.

You never heard of that fiddler.

I never heard such a pretty story all my life.

Sam Starr

She remembers mainly his height. He was a tall man like his daddy. Had a lot of brothers. Mean ones, the lot of them, but Sam was all right. She and Eddy were at the wedding of Sam and Belle. This would have been in '80 or thereabouts. There was lots of dancing, and this time she was allowed to join the sets. She danced with her cousin, little Wash Starr, who was big like all the Starrs, even at that age, maybe twelve or thirteen. He swung her hard, she remembers, and smelled like horsefeed.

Sam Starr was killed at a dance. They were after him for something or other and he was going to ride to Fort Smith rather than face the Lighthorsemen, but Frank West, one of them Lighthorsemen, was at the dance and they settled their grudge quick enough. Sam had his arms around a tree like he was trying to climb it and was shouting, Daddy, but you knew he was dying. Tom Starr stood over him and shook his head. Jim July laid Sam out flat and then the dance went on.

Not long after this Jim July took Sam's place.

The Arrest of Watson

We was the law unto ourselves mainly, like I was saying and so we done it ourselves. He came to the funeral, see, Watson stood there and watched, his hat in his hand, and I swear he was grinning. He done it. Sure, he was the one. Someone paid him to, that's my opinion. Judge Parker of Fort Smith, if you ask me. And there we was, me and Eddy and Jim July taking Watson to Parker's court for a hearing. It was Jim July's idea. At the funeral he says to Watson, you are under arrest. That right, says Watson. Jim July was going to get Eddy to help take Watson in, and I persuaded Eddy they needed my help too. It's no use, I said to Eddy, but I want to go to Fort Smith. I could get some shopping done there. Eddy said he didn't care what I did. So I went along.

It was like we was going on a little outing, the four of us taking a holiday to the springs, a picnic. I never saw Watson any friendlier, and Jim July brought along a flask of Catoosa gin that he passed back and forth. Soon it was dark and cold, this being February. I rode with Eddy, and, back behind us, Jim July rode with Watson. Eddy wasn't much company, riding along beside me not saying a word, staring at the trees, and I could hear Jim July and Watson back there chattering like they was trail buddies and now and then in the clearings when the moon shone bright I'd look back and see the flask pass between them like it was a little piece of light.

You go back and ride with Watson a while, I told Eddy. Send Jim July up here with me. I was lonesome. It was a lonesome night, all right, Eddy no company at all. He'd be a match for Watson though, I figured.

And I guess he was too. I rode with Jim July the rest of the way. You think they're all right back there, I'd say. Sure, says Jim, they're getting along fine. He told me a lot of things that night, but nary a word about Mama. He had a lot of grand ideas, did Jim July. I was surprised, because I'd always thought him crazy, just a little, with that long hair slicked back and hanging down to his shoulderblades, and he never, before then, had much to say, like most of Mama's men, silent and sneaky. That night, though, he talked and talked. He was going out to the Strip and raise cattle and build himself a town. He wanted a town with his name on it. He wanted people to remember him after he was gone. But first he was going to see that Watson was cut down to size.

We rode all night. Day was breaking when we come to the river. Jim July tried hard, but it wasn't no use. He couldn't even get Eddy to testify against Watson. It's no use, said Eddy. Told me later he thought nobody killed Mama. It had just come her time. He hadn't seen her like I did that day, her face down in the mud. Later he had a change of heart. After Jim July got killed by that young fellow Hutchins, Eddy swore he'd see justice done himself, and that was the end of him. Watson's been down in Atoka, he'd say. Frank Mayfield said he saw him coming out of the feedstore. And off Eddy'd go. Atoka one day, Poteau or Tahlequah or Tishomingo the next. Someone was always seeing Watson and telling Eddy about it. I think it got to be a joke after a time. Anytime someone'd see a stranger, they'd say, there goes Watson. Tell Eddy you seen Watson. But it was never Watson, not once.

The Meaning of Her Life

She has kept herself alive. She has outlived many that would have done her harm if they had half a chance. She has lived to see her Flossie married with a fine family, such as families go. She has kept going when others have burned theirselves into the ground. She has taken care of herself, no one else to do it for her, and she is proud of it.

It's the same world as it was back then, she says. Don't make no difference whether you ride a automobile or a horse. Folks coming and going, just like always, no more smart than we was.

She grins, passes me the whisky bottle.

Not as smart, she says. We knew where we was.

Where was that, I ask, laughing now, all that whisky.

We was in the Territory, she says.

In the Territory. She says it again. Indian Territory. There wasn't no place else to be. *It was the last place in the world.*

And it's the same now?

Damn right. Now you tell me *your* story, son.

But she rose, and I saw she meant to close the conversation.

THE FIDDLER

The old men sit on the steps of the council house whittling on small sticks, paring fingernails with jackknives, their jaws swollen with tobacco. They look up when he and Belle approach, but do not make way. Belle's foot is so fast that his first impression is of a snake jumping from beneath her long skirt. Knife and stick fly from the hands of the old man in the center, clattering against the sandstone and off into the dirt. The old men stand, rising at the same instant, straight as soldiers, and quickly move onto the grass. Inside, the chief, in his long-cut dark coat, striped trousers, vest, and string tie, greets Belle with a smile, extending his broad hand and then, embarrassed, withdrawing it. She turns to him, her companion of these many months, and says, You wait outside. This is a business meeting.

Waiting, he wonders: How is it that this man Byron comes to write poetry? Some of it amuses him, he has to admit, but where do such ideas come from, where does one man learn to use words in so unusual a manner, the rhymes making each line sound as though it could have been said in no other way? When *he* thinks, as now, everything seems all a-jumble. He might think of taking the cabriolet down to Tuskahoma or he might consider, weather permitting, a swim in the Fourche Maline. He might, on the other hand, recall the time he and Belle lay on the banks of the Kiamichi, the sun streaming down through the golden leaves, her skin glistening in the deep autumn light. Anything, it seems, can come to *his* mind. No logic to the order, never a rhyme, often nothing at all, the scent of Belle's soap lingering, the sound of her voice persistent as the wind in the trees, the caress of her hand soft as honeydew. *With you, Belle,* he thinks, *I'll gladly go to—anywhere!*

His rival approaches. The man smiles, tips his broad-brimmed hat. Mounting his shiny horse, he says: I'm thinking it's about time you moved on, fiddler. This country ain't no place for the likes of you. You stay around and I'm afraid something bad might happen to you. I hear tell some folks around here have taken a dislike to you. I think you'd best move on.

These are times, she tells him, when it is exciting to be alive. The unassigned lands to the west of the Indian Nations will be settled soon, the great cattle trails give way to railroads, fresh new cities, prosperous farms. When that time comes he will have a chance to make a new life for himself. He will no longer need Belle, his manhood opening before him like a railroad bed through unexplored territory. Don't cling to me, she says, think big. It's a big land, big fortunes to be made. Honesty don't always pay. Get yourself a dream and go to it. My way ain't necessarily the best way. I've got my regrets. But I am a woman and you are a man. You have advantages therefore. Buy when the price is low, sell when it's high. Go after what you want, *but make sure that what you want is worth what it takes to get it!*

She has known the Confederate guerrilla chief Quantrill, the James Boys, the Youngers. Of Jesse James she says: He is the handsomest man I have ever known, present company excepted. He has blue eyes, deep blue just like a baby's and a smile pretty as any woman's. That boy can charm the skin off of a rattler. And let me tell you what those Pinkertons did. They threw a fire bomb into his mother's house that killed her littlest boy, blew a hole in his side big enough to stick your hand through and tore up her arm so bad it had to be cut off. Her right arm. It was the

Pinkertons and nothing ever came of it. Those bastards are still drawing their paychecks, you bet. He has heard the story many times. Afterwards she looks at him and the tears are big in her eyes. Play me that fiddle, she says. Play me the Soldiers' Joy.

She will come to a violent end. In dreams he has already seen it happen. She is in the caves surrounded by men with long-barreled rifles gripped firmly in their thick hands and ammunition belts strapped tightly around their chests. You might as well give up, Belle, their leader shouts. You can't last forever. She hands him small round pebbles. Throw, she says. Bullets whine, echo, chip away at the cave wall. Twice-hit, her arms bandaged from wrist to shoulder, with the toe of her boot she dislodges stones from the damp floor of the cave and kicks them out the mouth down the steep slope. It is only a matter of time. He tosses the little rocks furiously.

Belle wakes him. She is lonely. She wants to be touched. She says: Listen to the wind in the trees, how it thrills the leaves. Listen to the faraway stars, to the hootowl, to the sparrowhawk, to the pine needles falling. Listen to the waters of the river washing over the smooth stones. She wants him to know how the fish darting from eddy to eddy in and out of the jutting rocks look like his fingers when, as in moments such as these, he comes to her, his skin warming, his blood riled. Oh, Lord, she says. *Oh, Lord!*

He wakes hearing the hoofbeats but is not sure at first whether they are going away or coming closer. Then he hears the rebel yell, piercing and wild, one voice followed by a clatter of shouts and cheers. Belle! She is not there. She has risen while he slept. He starts to get up, but no, she will not want him with her. He listens to the loud voices, hears her laughter above the tumult, her own shouts as spirited as the men's but distinct from theirs, a woman's voice without doubt. She won't come back to him tonight, that much he knows.

He is with Belle, lying in a bed of pine needles. He can hear the swift waters of the river—it would be the Canadian—and the sky above them is as blue, surely, as the eyes of Jesse James. Sometimes, she says, I am no more here with you than that hawk is wishing a long life for field mice. The war is still going on. I'm in Missouri and Charley Quantrill is looking at me and saying, One hundred and eighty-two, Belle. We got us one hundred and eighty-two Jayhawkers in Lawrence. Lined 'em up in the streets and shot 'em dead. And Charley so pale and refined. Used to be a schoolteacher. He had a way of looking at you that cut to the bone, like he knew he could slash your throat if he took a notion to and was considering whether he might just do it. For spite. Because he knew he *could* do it, had done just as sorry a deed more than once, and it didn't matter to him whether you deserved it or not. Maybe better if you didn't deserve it. And we all looked up to Charley Quantrill. Oh, yes, we did. He had no fear, you see. He was absolutely *without fear*.

This is rugged, mountainous country, the sunsets often turning the mist rising from the riverbottoms into wild and ragged clouds. In the valleys of the Kiamichi and the Clear Boggy and the Red, the Choctaws have built towns and farmhouses, leasing the rocky and hilly backwoods lands to the many former slaves that roam the territory or to whites from Arkansas or Texas who are able to purchase work permits or marry into the tribe. His idea has been to find a Choctaw bride. Arriving in Doaksville, in the Apukshunnubbee District, the southern section near the Red River, he applies for his work permit. At the desk of the hotel a dark-eyed woman hands him the quill. Don't think it will be easy, she says. Nothing is easy in Apukshunnubbee. The old men are in control. Gradually he drifts north, his fiddle case strapped to his back like a small coffin, comes to Antlers, crosses the Winding Stair Mountains, follows the Muddy Boggy to Atoka, the Butterfield route to Buffalo Station, Pulsey's Station, Riddle's. The shabby hillside farms, the gaunt faces, the glinting eyes so quick to look away, all sadden him.

West of the cross-timbers the short-grass country seems to stretch out, flat and treeless, to the end of the earth. Out there, Belle says, you've got real Indians. Cheyenne, Arapaho, Comanche, Kiowa. Nothing like these beaten-down Choctaw, who need federal soldiers to protect them. She likes the Cheyenne best. They live and breathe war. Little Wolf and Dull Knife, great chiefs, will not long be kept on the southern range, you bet, will lead their people back to the northern lands right across Kansas and Nebraska, soldiers and settlers be damned, you wait and see. Once a Cheyenne makes up his mind to do something, he won't be stopped. You'll have to kill him first.

The blacks, freedmen of the old Choctaw chiefs, come in to Tuskahoma from the meager and rocky fields. They are not liked by the old men at the council house, who make a show of spitting whenever one of them walks up to the door, and they do not stay long in town. He feels a kinship to these blacks and imagines that he might befriend one some day and learn some of their secrets. One of them pays regular visits to Belle, a young woman, very dark, very supple, long-boned and lean, her skirts so tight that her hips and thighs seem merely painted in curious patterns designed to absorb light and reflect shadow in the most happy of ways. She steps briskly past him, no hesitation, no elaborate shuffling to one side the way the black men in Tuskahoma do in the presence of the old Choctaw men, moving swiftly beyond him, leaving an aroma both sweet and briefly tart, as though of pine needles and dogwood blossoms and maybe a little of the bark of jackoaks. He hears Belle greet her with a boisterous shout and then the two women laugh and their voices are steady, he can't tell them apart, diminishing to a throaty whispering and then at last to no sound at all. Instead, an occasional series of quick footsteps, a creaking floorboard, a window wrenched open, slammed shut.

There have been other men besides himself. She retains keepsakes. On her chiffonier is a red hatband, much frayed around the edges, a long white feather sewn into it at the side. On the oak bedstand is an ivory-handled straight razor, initialed *J.R.*, under the bed a pair of Mexican boots of large size. Try them on, she says one day, tossing him one of the heavy boots, but they are too large. J.R. is dead, shot down in Texas. Others, however, live. Tall men, dust-coated and breathless, ride up, jump down from their dark, sweaty horses and call out: Belle! Belle, honey! Belle, you got company, now come down here! One of them stays for weeks, Belle nursing his slight wounds as though he might otherwise die, bathing him nightly. Another comes calling regularly. This one worries him. The man is from the other side of the Canadian in the Cherokee Nation, a mixed blood, his father half Irish, half Cherokee. He has dark eyes and broad shoulders, wears silk shirts, a flat-brimmed black stetson, shining snub-toed boots, and takes her for long walks along the Fourche Maline. Oh, Belle, the man says, one of these days I'm going to make an honest woman of you.

It has been an unusually long winter. Belle is restless. She wants her Byron every evening. They sit in the soft glow of the kerosene lamps, she in the horsehair armchair, her voluminous skirt tucked under her, he in the rocker, rocking to the rhythm of the rhymed lines. Afterwards he likes to walk in the frozen fields, consider beneath the bright stars and the moonlight the direction his life will take when it is all over with Belle. He thinks perhaps he will leave the territory altogether, go to St. Joe or Kansas City. He sees himself aboard the train, lulled to sleep by the clacking of the rails, the warm sunshine through the windows. Wake up, sir, the porter says, here is your stop. Why, so it is! The air on the station platform is brisk but not chilling. He takes a deep breath, approaches a large, ruddy-cheeked man in a checkered waistcoat, offers a cigar, says: I'm looking out for a position in your fair city. Can you maybe offer advice? The man claps him heartily on the back. I've got just the thing for a young man like you!

How did he take up with Belle. He sees her one day in town. He is farming on Choctaw land and has come in to purchase seed. She stands before him on the plank walk, one leg propped on the watering trough, her boots spattered with red clay, her hair pulled up high on her head in two thickly coiled braids. She stares straight ahead, seems intently studying the exact position of each horse, memorizing the slant of the corrugated tin rooftops across the way. He steps around her and into the store. When he comes out she is in the same place, but now everything on the other side of the road is bathed in an orange glow such as he has never seen before, the sky behind the frame buildings a purple close enough to touch. Ain't that lovely, Belle says. He sees that there are tears in her eyes.

She cannot stomach the winter. I'm going south, she says. I'm going down to Texas, to Abilene, Austin, Brownsville. Going to disguise myself. Lend me your hat, your trousers, your silver-tipped cane. No, he says, it will never work. To his surprise she says no more about it. She sits for hours in front of the fire, rubbing her hands, almost touching her toes to the crackling flame. He kneels beside her, the worn volume of Byron in his hand. No, she says, not tonight. Tonight I am not here. I am in the fire. Keep away unless you want to be burned.

They are riding through the pine forests in the cabriolet. Belle is talkative, in high spirits. She speaks of her childhood in

Missouri, how as a little girl she liked to hide in the stable. One day, she says, I had the feeling that the sides of the stable were closing in on me. Everything was dark and still. The horses didn't even seem to swish their tails. I thought they were holding their breath, like they heard something, smelled something, knew something. But I wasn't afraid. This is the strange part. I knew I should have been afraid, but instead I was happy, shaking all over so much I knew I couldn't stand up, and still it kept getting darker and the walls coming in closer, and now there was a crow cawing somewhere and I was laughing. I had to laugh, not because anything was funny but because I was so happy and the crow's caw was so sweet. That was it—it was so *sweet!* And at the same time I remember thinking, Belle, you had better come out of this, this is surely not right feeling this way. I don't know how long it lasted. I didn't want it to stop, not really, even while I was telling myself it had to and I had to make it, but it did stop and I stood up at last, my legs weak and still shaking, and walked back to the house. I went back to the stable—a lot of times after that—but it never happened again. I wish it did.

She can be sultry. Paint my lips, she says, and he obliges, opening the jar of red cream, touching the thick paste with the tip of his little finger, dabbing the lips lightly with quick short strokes while her tongue darts in and out. Later she asks him to read to her from the Lord Byron set. Anything, she says. With him it's six of one and a half a dozen of the other. Sometimes he walks out into the fields, to the riverbottom, wades in the shallow water, goes to the big rock overhang and plays his fiddle to the stars. At the corral he strokes the noses of the horses, who neigh gently and then, eager for sugar, nuzzle the palm of his hand, their mouths warm and wet like food.

He considers riding north into Missouri, looking for Frank and Jesse James, the Youngers. Walking through cornfields he listens for the clicking of their revolvers. Charley Quantrill, dead these ten years, will come to him in a dream and say, Now I'm going to show you the hideout. He lies beneath the stars, waiting for that instructive sleep. Frank, Belle says, can quote you Shakespeare lickety-split, and Jesse sing Baptist hymns in as sweet and strong a voice as you've ever heard, his blue eyes beaming. With Jesse and Frank and Cole and Bob and Jim he will ride for days across the hot plains, the wind in his face warm, stinging, ahead of them nothing but banks, trains, and stagecoaches teeming with treasures. Afraid for their lives, old men give away their watches, their tightly rolled bundles of banknotes, beautiful women their shining jewels, their secret keepsakes. At the camp at night Jesse sings *The Old Rugged Cross,* moving them all to tears.

The idea of respectability is not by any means ridiculed by Belle. Often she speaks to him of her admiration of the farmwives, of women who bear children and raise them to be decent and hardworking citizens, of women who stand by their husbands' side "through thick and thin," encourage virtue, scorn sin, of women who care for orphans, feed the poor, cure the ill. She would do it all if she were able. Here her voice falters. He takes her in his arms. I want it all, she says. I want to be everyone at once. I want everything to happen to me.

She likes to hold the fiddle. The shape, the smoothness of the wood and its rippling grain, the narrow tapering neck, the scroll with its delicate carved circles, all appeal to her. Where does it come from, she wonders. He tells her it has been called the devil's box, but he doesn't know who made the first one, where it was played. Across the ocean, he says. A long time ago. She takes a soft cloth and rubs the wood, bringing the dark curly-maple back and sides to a high sheen, then rubbing the spruce top. There, she says, play hell out of it.

She likes to dance. He likes to watch her while he pulls the bow in a cloud of rosin-dust across the strings. In the Grand Promenade she steps with a fluid speed and delicacy to the sweet whine of the fiddle, the thrumming chords of the guitar, moving as though the music might echo the rhythm of her heart's strokes and vein-throbs. *Hi-Yi!* she shouts during the Virginia Reel. She pulls her partner, his rival, along through the clapping lines of dancers, her forehead perspiring, shining soft as moonlight in the dim lampglow of the dancehall, her heels rapping time against the hardwood floor, her long dark skirt whirling one way then another as though it were a great calico pinwheel blown by shifting winds. Moments like these, he thinks later, one does not need anything else in the world. We come together in air, coaxed out of ourselves for an instant of eternity, not let loose from our senses so much as living altogether inside them, the tingling in our fingertips and the sweet dust on our tongues the very feel and taste of life past and to come. He strokes that fiddle.

The men ride up hollering and hooting. *Belle, Belle!* She shakes her head, looks at him, smiling, takes his hand and kisses it. He is not certain how to read that look. Does she regret what she is about to do? Wish she might stay here with him? All she says is, It's time. For weeks she prepares, packing carefully in her big trunk the fine gowns, the riding breeches, the pearl-inlaid fans, the lace mantillas, the colorful bandanas. Afternoons he hears the sharp explosions of the Winchester, the ring of the empty shells against the stones. At meals she is silent, her eyes lowered, and he knows not to try to make conversation, not to ask: Where this time? How long? When will this end? She stops attending dances. Frivolous entertainments, she says. He plays with abandon, but the figures dance before him like so many rag dolls, gaily dressed but no blood throbbing, and the bow scrapes across the strings as though intending harm. *It's time!*

Belle gone, he wanders. He takes long rides, sometimes in the cabriolet, sometimes astride the dappled mare. One day, walking, he carries his fiddle with him. At the creekbank, the water running clear in its curving corridors, the little fish shining among the clean stones, he takes the fiddle and bow out of the case and plays the sweet airs from the old country. Then after a time, fiddle again in its black case, he climbs to the caves, up the steep sandstone and into the mouth, dark and cool, the air thick, almost liquid. The first wide inner room gives way to narrow passageways that wind and descend deep into the mountain, the rockfloors smooth with sometimes a jagged edge rising. His eyes adjusted to the dark, he has the sense of a close but unfolding grayness, as though he strolled through a stormcloud. He places his fiddle, still in its case, on a ledge jutting perhaps a foot outwards at head height, deep back in the caverns, then makes his way again towards the light, the swaying pines, the river, down broad paths towards the valleys and towns.

He comes back. He is playing for her at the caves, as she often likes him to do on the long summer nights. Never does his fiddle sound more quick with its ringing high notes, more tremolant in the lower registers. She is inside, sitting in the darkness, he standing just at the entranceway, the large white stones reflecting the moonlight as though by design. On this night she prefers the sweet, slow airs, has him play one after the other. It is still when he starts to play, but soon wind begins to blow through the pine needles, rustling them, and he has the feeling that this wind carries the sound of his fiddle over the trees and down into the frame houses along the valleys of the Fourche Maline. He is no longer the fiddler, but the music itself, and Belle inside the cave no human listener, the soft earth's ear. In the black sky long slivers of clouds that resemble blades of grass seem to pause and stroke the swaying tops of the trees before they move on across and beyond the distant dark ridges. He will love her forever.

JIM REED

Belle stands by his side, firing so fast that it seems to him she aims for a regiment. He sees nothing out there. Pull your pistol, Jim, she says. Don't let me down. His pistol's gone. In the holster he finds a large unhusked ear of corn. It's all I got, he tells her. Throw it at them, she says. He throws. There's an explosion. That's the way, she says. Now we've got them where we want them.

Some dream, he'd say, waking.

He likes best the waiting, watching, thinking about how it'll be when he rides into town with Clell and Bill, everybody at their places, Cole usually the one to go into the bank, do the talking. The townsfolk don't know nothing, but you know they're likely to figure out what's what and then is when the real kick comes. You have to think fast, mount fast, ride fast, maybe shoot fast, and the dust starts tasting thick enough to chew. You can get your horse shot from under you, like Payne Jones one time. And if you're caught, like as not you'll get no trial, just a rope. Dick Burns went that way, and McGuire, and Tom Little. He thinks about the rope too, how it'd feel when they tighten it around your neck, the bristles rubbing, the horse restless beneath you. They take a willow switch and swipe it across the horse's flanks. What happens next is anybody's guess.

Marrying Belle he has imagined that his life is just beginning. Charley Quantrill's no more, the war's over. Next to the burned houses new ones are building, their foundations of white Missouri stone. It's good, says Belle. You and me together, we're all right, ain't we. Jim, she says, I'm going to show you a thing or two, and by damn she does! Where has she learned, he wonders.

They walk near the caves. He hears the water in the Fourche Maline, the wind in the pines, and then something else that he can't at first figure out, a wailing but no human voice. It chills him. Belle walks a steady brisk pace, her boots not even kicking up dust. She takes his hand. Ain't that pretty, she says. What? he asks. That music, she says. Coming from the caves. Then he knows. It's the fiddler, up there in the rocks playing that damn fiddle. Jim, Belle says, that music does something to me. Let's stop. Let's set a spell. Here. Look here at this nice clearing. Let's just set a spell and rest. She talks soft, sure, but very near drags him to the ground. Damn that fiddler though! Why can't he play something with a little spirit to it, something fast, if he has to play.

While he's gone, the fiddler comes and plays for her. He knows this for a fact. I like him and his music, Belle says. He's someone I can talk to. We take walks down along the Fourche Maline. He likes to walk. Carries his fiddle. We stop at a sunny rock and he takes the fiddle out and plays. I like the sound of the fiddle with the wind playing in the leaves and the water gliding in the river. Do you dance there too, he asks. Yes, she says. Sometimes I do. And other times? I just listen. I lie down on the rock in the sunshine. I listen, warmed by the music and the sun.

Jesse is out in California looking for his father's grave. Frank too. Belle says, Jim, is your father living. Yes, he says, far as I know. He doesn't care to know. He remembers a big man, bald and with bright black eyes, coming for him from out of the high weeds and rocks, saying, Boy, come out of there. If I have to find you I'm gonna whip you good. Whip him anyway, whether he comes out or stays hid, and so he waits stretched out belly down against the soft ground near the creekbed, waits because that way she goes into the cave and the man kneels, takes the fiddle out of its case. From down here the man looks small, but he is not. The fiddle must be magic to make such sounds.

The man says, Here you can hold it. It's all right. Yes, she says, you can if you want to. Just don't drop it. It's not as heavy as he expects it to be. The wood seems hard like the marble top of her dresser, but you can see beneath the shininess to the softer part where there are dark shapes like wings. Like this, the man says, pressing its thick end into his neck. Squeeze down on it with your chin and put your hand up here. The trees are making a lot of noise, they sound like many small birds singing at once. It is dark out there. She sits on the porch in her white dress, her face lit by the light from the window. The man is bending down to him, putting the bow in his hand.

He lets the water touch his chin. This is as deep as it goes, but he can make it come higher by bending his knees, and when he sits down all the water is above him, white where the sky touches it. He can hold his breath for a long time and keep his eyes open and listen to the singing far away. In town the old men—Choctaw, she says—come towards him when she is in the building, some of them with canes, their hands curled around the thick tips of the sticks. He hears them humming to themselves. They don't mean for him to hear them. He sits beneath the tree in the shade, watching the door. Soon it will open.

She keeps the pistol in a wooden box in one of the drawers. He lifts the box carefully and sets it down. Also in the drawer are bright-colored pieces of cloth cut in many shapes, long strips and circles and squares, some of the pieces made of a thick furry cloth that feels good rubbed against your cheek, touched to your lips. There are ribbons, these shiny and not thick at all, red and yellow and blue, and at the very back of the drawer three spools of live in. It'll not be the same for you. This land is going to be opened up. You'll have a chance.

The shells are warm when they fall in the dirt. It is all right for him to pick them up and keep them. She holds the pistol straight out, her arm not moving at all until after the explosion and then only a little bounce in the air, her bright-colored scarves blowing in the wind like flags. He is ready for the land to open up, says, When it happens will we fall very far, and she laughs, says, No, it's not that kind of opening, and she explains so that he sees what she means, a time when the Indian lands in the west can be settled by people like him who will work hard to improve it, build homes much better than this one, plant and harvest crops.

In her mirror his face does not seem his own. He doesn't know whose it is. He sits before the mirror and touches the marble top of the dresser, takes her big comb and runs it through his hair the way he has seen her do hers. His hair has been long like hers. Now, she says, it is time to cut it. You are getting to be a big boy, Eddy, do you know that? He remembers that it doesn't hurt when hair is cut. She saves some of his, has it in a box, and sometimes he takes it out to look at. It feels soft like hers, and he thinks it really is hers and not his hair at all, or that maybe she is mistaken and it is his sister's hair. The hair on his head feels stiff and does not shine like this hair she keeps in the box, tied with a yellow ribbon.

He wades out into the water until it comes to his shoulders. The current is not so strong here and the water at his feet is very cool, the sand soft like mud coming up between his toes and covering them over until he takes another step. They can't see him from the cave. Even if they knew he was there and were looking for him down here they could not see him. But he can see them. He can see her climbing the rocks, the man not far behind. The moonlight is bright, but it shines on them and not on him. Now place where the ground is smooth and hard and hidden by thick clusters of bushes with bright leaves.

He keeps an eye on the pistol. There is a hollowed-out place on the rock where it can safely wait, no risk of its falling into the water, where he can still see it shining close by him. The water flows cool and swift and the round slick stones at the bottom move only a little when his toes touch them. When she is gone, the pistol goes with her. She carries it in a fine leather holster strapped tight around her waist. She lets him put the pistol in its place because he has been good and has promised to be a man when she is gone. He is going to be a grand and brave man, she tells him, and some day a woman will love him and he will make that woman very happy. Near her the smell is pleasant, the air better to breathe, and so he breathes it into him deep as he can and fast so that he will get more of it. He likes to run his hand across the top of her dresser, but it is not as good as the holster. She says, Do you like that? Well, here, come here and try it on for size. She pulls it to the last notch, says, Oh, it's too big, and laughs, drawing him into her arms. Mama's big boy. Mama's sweet Eddy.

The water darkens where it runs deeper, but it is not so swift and the feel of the stones giving way to sand is very nice. The barrel of the pistol points away from the river towards the tall trees. The man makes the fiddle sound sad, though it is a long way away and the sound of it mixed with that of the trees and the birds and the sky. Sometimes the men invite him to sit on their laps, but the fiddler only wants to shake his hand and does not squeeze it hard like Mr. Starr, but holds it as though he only wants to know how heavy it is. She tells him that Jesse James once held him on his lap and sang a hymn for him and that some day he will want to tell that story to his children. Who is Jesse James, he wants to know. She says, Some say an outlaw, but a real gentleman I say, a good and brave man. These are hard times we

EDDY THE BOY

He runs all the way to the river. It's a hot day. She calls after him, but no matter. She won't come this far. The man won't either. The man will take the fiddle out of its dark case and, still standing, play it for her while she sits on the porch. He takes off his shirt, folds it. The rock is hot against his bare feet. He sets down the pistol next to the shirt on the rock so that the sun can warm it. It is all right that he has it. She has said that he might hold it and that some day she will teach him to shoot it so that he can hit even the fastest targets. She keeps the pistol clean. He watches her hold it in her lap and rub the handle with a soft cloth. She sings softly—to herself, but he always listens, likes to hear her hum those tunes the fiddler plays, the slow, sad ones she has him play for her when they go across the river to the caves.

At the caves the rocks are cool. In her white dress and good leather boots, her long hair tucked up under a broad-brimmed hat tied with a veil under her chin, she climbs easily, shunning the help of the fiddler. Trees sway, pines, he thinks these are pines, yes, pines, they have needles, soft and brown beneath their trunks to lie down upon. She climbs easily. The man carries the fiddle in a black box with part of a belt for a handle. *Looks like a little coffin, don't it. I made it that way on purpose.* He can only see the man up there. She is inside the cave, or in the dark part back just far enough to make her hidden. The man stands facing the mouth of the cave, his fiddle sticking out from his chest, a small dark thing from where he watches among the trees at the that Sam Starr? No sign of him here, that's for sure. Just Belle, sitting on that smooth white rock, sun pushing through the trees and lighting up her skin. She turns. Why, Jim. Morning, honey.

Would this woman cheat on him? Time a-plenty to think on that later.

Belle will live long after him. His own death he feels comes close now. The wind blows him back into himself. He is a bad man, a mean man. The world will not miss him. His mother's voice whispers to him in the wind: *Jim Reed, you ain't no son of mine*. Ain't nobody's son. Sprouted from a seed in the dirt. Touch him, you might as well touch a tree. Hard, yes, he's a hard, mean man, don't take nothing from nobody. Rides alone. Belle can't save him. He wishes it might be different, sure, and sometimes, lying with her out under the stars, knowing she is there beside him breathing and dreaming and warm, he thinks God damn it is different and he is not Jim Reed but someone else, someone clean and good and new, the hot tears rolling down his cheeks bearing away the soul of that old Jim, yes, that soul streaming down from his eyes and the moon shining down on him like it meant it. Lasts about a minute. Tears turn cold on his cheeks, dry fast. Belle, turning to him in her sleep, cries out. He can't understand what she's said. Soon he's drowsy, closes his eyes. Quantrill is there, pacing the cornfields. Jim, he says. Jim Reed. Looky here, Jim. Here's that fiddler's hand. Take it to Belle. Hurry now! She's waiting for you. Right up there in the caves. That's where she is. Inside the caves, waiting for you. Hurry now. *Git!* The hand is warm, its fingers pressing against his wrist. Lighting out for the hideout in the caves, he hangs onto that hand hard.

and the rushes that you think they must have always been there, old as them smooth flat rocks. From the tips of some of the white cones smoke rises, and the leaves of the cottonwoods flicker in the wind, the sun shining off the white backs of the leaves. It's too clear now, and he wants to ride away fast, but Sam says no, they don't see us, won't so long as we keep a good distance, ride slow down back of that stand of jackoaks and then over that little bluff.

He's not sure. Feels like they're watching, they're all around, hidden and watching. Beyond the bluff he feels better, but then they come to a platform, like a high table made with thick tall branches for legs. A burial scaffold. The dark mound on top is a dead Cheyenne. Beneath lies the horse killed for riding in the next world. The smell is like spoiled meat. He feels a chill, wants to get away from here fast. Might be a good rifle up there, Sam says. A lot of times they leave his favorite rifle. But he makes no move to go look. Come on, Belle says. We got plenty of territory to cover before night.

One morning he wakes and Belle is not there. Neither is Sam Starr. It's already warm, though still early, the sun just above the tree line making long shadows across the camp, no wind blowing and the birds singing loud. The others still sleep, sun not yet shining on their faces. He crosses the clearing, enters the stand of cottonwoods, angles through the prickly brambles to the creekbank. There she is, kneeling, the clear water flowing through her hair. He listens for snapping twigs, footsteps, but only hears the birds, the creekwater washing over the rocks, and Belle's humming. Now, pulling her head up and back so that the long hair hangs in thick strands dripping down her back and across her bare shoulders, she begins to sing: *Swing low, sweet chariot*—and pulls a black comb through her hair, short quick thrusts first, then long slow easy strokes, the hair shining like all get-out. Where is

Just a minute, boys. Hold on.

She has pulled her horse to a stop just at the edge of a long barren butte. Look out there, she says. Tell me what you see. He sees a long stretch of dry treeless land, flat save where slashed by a ravine or gully, out in the distance a winding creekbed of red sand. The sky's as much white as blue, with silver-edged clouds starting to climb up high in the northwest over the edge of the flat land.

What I see, Belle says, is a city. Big as Saint Louis, spread out miles and miles and surrounded by acres of farmland, land that is teeming with wheat fields and apple orchards.

Belle, you got to have water first. And where are all them people going to come from?

Kansas. Texas, Missouri. I-o-way. All over.

They going to bring the water with them?

She looks out there, her horse still as though he too is trying to picture it. I don't know, says Sam. The way I see it, just about anything can happen. People need water, they'll get it.

Belle smiles. *Wheat and apples*. She gives her horse a light swish with the reins, rides on ahead, down toward the bowl-shaped buffalo wallows and the dry creekbeds of the plains.

It's always a strong wind. The dust, red and thick, stirs first along the bottoms. He watches it rise and spread, the blue-white sky reddening. There, says Sam, there they come. But he's wrong. There's no cattle coming yet, just the wind up to its tricks. Sam breathes deep, pulls his bandana up. Git them horses, he says. And so they ride fast down the slope into the red air, cheeks stinging with the hardblown dust, and find no cattle, nothing at all, Sam still gasping for breath, looking around like he still thinks the cattle's there somewhere, only hid away, some trick.

In the distance the tipis of the Cheyenne wind along the banks of the river, rows of them so neatly placed among the cottonwoods

Poor Jim—
Jim who.
You Jim. My Jim Reed.
Pity's not what I want.
No. I guess I know what you want.
What's that.
What I give you.

Gone for months, Jesse comes riding up out of breath, his face red like the dust. He talks less than he used to, makes fewer jokes. He's sick at heart, Belle says. Wants to settle, marry that little cousin of his up in Kansas City and raise him a family. He's a good man, a decent man. Just had no luck.

Jesse sits before the fire, staring at it, jabbing at it now and then with a poker. He's had hard times, Belle says. Haven't we all. Yes, Belle says, but he's had harder than most. Jesse turns and looks at them, blue eyes blinking. Listen here, he says, it's a good life. A damn good life. Ain't nobody good enough for it, that's all. He turns back to the fire, shuts up. After a while, beds down for the night.

Such tiny feet, Belle whispers. Such small white hands.

Jim Reed needs death to come sudden. A bullet in the back of the neck. He wants to be in the middle, riding fast and not falling from that saddle, his horse speeding him into the woods. Dead, sitting straight in the saddle and holding tight to the reins, he can't see, no, but he can feel the wind, strong and hot, stealing him away to hell, and he can hear Quantrill saying, You and me and Anderson, we're going to show them how to kill Jayhawkers. Going to line them up and shoot them one by one square in the skull.

Hell's coming that way. Come on, then.

of her. She won't let him touch her on these trips. No, sir. And he wants her bad. But he's proud all the same. At camp she builds the fire. Later she jokes around.

Belle, he says, that fire don't need all that care. It's doing just fine. Come here and let me warm you. She don't answer, stays by the fire. Sam Starr says, Maybe she's missing the old homestead, and she turns around for sure then. Sam gets her coffee — probably not hot for all the time she's been sipping at it — splashed full in his face. What'd I say? he asks. Belle still won't talk. Not this night. Feisty, ain't she, Sam says. Jim tells him he better say no more. When she gets this way, no telling what'll come next. I like a feisty woman, says Sam.

A man like that, Belle says, a man like that, he's different, ain't he.

What man do you mean, Belle.

Jim. I'm talking about Jim.

Jim. *I'm* Jim, honey.

Jim the fiddler. You know who I mean.

I'm Jim. Just call him the fiddler, okay.

All right. The fiddler. That's who I'm talking about.

What about him.

He's different. You know what I mean?

Yeah, he plays the fiddle.

It's *how* he plays. What happens when he plays. Like he's not in this world anymore.

I notice you like his fiddling all right.

Yes.

Him too.

Yes, because he *is* the music. That's why. He pushes loose from himself soon's his fingers light on the strings. He is just not there.

Good riddance.

hands moving like they got minds of their own. Looks at Belle, does Charley Quantrill, smiles.

Why does he have such dreams, that's what he'd like to know.

He doesn't care for this country. Belle's idea to leave Texas. He'd go with her anywhere, but doesn't care for these red Indians that think they are good as white, hogging the good riverbottom land in their frame houses, busting the sod and raising up schools, acting like they think this land is theirs forever. Belle says, Hell, I know how to get along with them.

Can he trust her? Jesse comes and her eyes light up like she's just sat down on something that feels good. Says, well, look who's here. Jesse's eyes start blinking and his mouth opens wide but no words come out, nothing but air, his lungs gone bad, shot through while he was down in Texas with George Shepherd. Just a boy then, riled but not much count. Ain't no boy now, and Belle knows it, you can hear it in her voice, see it in the way she sidles up to Jesse and touches his sleeve.

You ever notice, Belle asks, Jesse's hands?

You mean how he's missing part of a finger?

Never noticed.

Delicate hands. Smooth and white. Hands are like eyes. They tell you about a person's character. Hands like Jesse's are unusual. They're the hands of a good man, a gentle man.

Rode with Charley Quantrill, same as you and me.

He's got little feet too. Tiny.

This time they are down in Texas. Belle keeps up with the rest of them just fine. He likes to watch her ride. She has a nice bounce in the saddle when they gallop down into the ravines. With her hair tucked up under her stetson, her pants riding low like a man's, her leather vest and black string tie, that Colt navy strapped tight, she looks like one of them all right, and he's proud wings spread high and wide. Handles the red fiddle gentle, passing it to Belle to hold while he takes the bow and, propping one end of it against the inside of his thigh, starts to rub it with rosin, short quick strokes then long smooth ones, Belle watching him and grinning. Finally this fellow takes the fiddle back from her and tucks it up by his chin, draws the bow across the strings while turning the black pegs, making the strings sound like they hurt. When he touches the strings with his long fingers, the bow starts to move lickety-split in short strokes and by God if he ain't playing a tune, maybe it's that Cotton Eye Joe. Belle's feet start to jumping and the fiddle eases down low on the fiddler's chest and he plays, sings:

> *Rise you up my dearest dear*
> *And present to me your hand*
> *And we'll go in pursuit*
> *Of some far and better land*
> *Where the hawk'll chase the buzzard*
> *And the buzzard'll chase the crow*
> *And we'll rally round the cane brake*
> *And chase the buffalo.*

Stroking long notes while he's singing, drawing the bow from one end to the other, then when he's got all the verses out, there he goes again with the short strokes and Belle's hopping like she's gone crazy, her arms swinging at her sides. Right there in broad daylight. Damndest thing you ever see!

Charley Quantrill comes up behind him, his footsteps quick and loud on the plank sidewalk. Jim, he says, Jim Reed. Kentucky's where we've got to go. I feel it in my bones. The war's in the East, not out here in Missouri. Hundreds of men, it'll be like Lawrence again.

Looks at you with those eyes of his, too dark, too happy, his

his father will know it won't be easy and maybe one of these days he'll be big enough and smart enough to wait and then come up on the old man from behind, say, Here I am and you have come after me for the last time. Belle says, I miss my papa sometimes, but not much, and my mama can go to hell all I care.

Of Tom Starr, Sam Starr says, My father's a greatly feared man. The Nation had to make a treaty with him and pay him off to keep him from making more trouble. It was like a war in those days, him against all the rest of the Nation. What started it was the treaties. That was a long time ago, when part of the Nation was in the East and part in the West. My father holds a grudge, but now they've paid him off and made a treaty with him and he says Tom Starr will kill no more. What he tells me is, Always do what you say you're going to do. Keep your word, Son, because it may be the only thing you got that you *can* keep.

The fiddler is a skinny, pale fellow, sunk-chested, eyes punched back deep in the hollows of a sallow face. Maybe he's thirty, maybe fifty, you can't say just how old. Plays down in Tuskahoma in the Choctaw Nation where they've leased him a patch of bottom land for the favor. In town he's always got that little black fiddle case along with him, like it's stuck onto his hand. Wears a broad-brim black hat, no crease nor fold in the crown, same way as the old Choctaw wear them, same kind of a hat, U.S. issue. Looks at you like he has never seen the likes before. Looks at Belle and them dark eyes open wide and a smile opens like a dent in his face, breath seeping out of him steady as water through a flour-plugged sieve. Get that fiddle out, Belle says, and play something before you fall over. And he snaps open that black case, pulls out a fiddle varnished red, shining like the dickens, a puff of white rosin like creekbank dust smack in the middle between the two curly slits in the top, on the back a painted picture of an eagle with yellow thread. The pistol is wrapped in soft red cloth and is heavy, but he can hold it easily, lift it in front of him the same way she does and keep his arm straight, keep his eye on the barrel of the pistol, pull the trigger if he wants to. The men tell him that they will show him how to hit the target. One of these days, she says.

Now, the man says, you just draw the bow across the strings, not too hard, that's the way. Now you're learning. The sound is not the same as when the man does it. He wants to stop it, but she says, My, ain't that fine, and he says, Do it again now. She is smiling and looks very happy, a breeze making her hair flow just a little to one side, covering part of her cheek and forehead. She looks pretty. The man's fingers, long and thin and strong, close around his hand. Press the string, he says. Press down hard on it and hold it there.

When he comes up the trees are swaying, the long branches high above moving up and down, the pine needles clustered thick and soft like hair. A red bird lights on the rock, flies quickly away. The pistol is safe. It has not been moved. She keeps the holster in the big chest, tucked between the folded sheets and the pretty dress she says she was wearing on her wedding day. There is a picture of his sister, but it doesn't look like her. The leather darkens where the pistol goes in and fits snug. He pulls the strap tight through the silver buckle and lets the pistol slide easily into its place, keeping his hand on the side of the handle until the very last and then with his palm pressing it the rest of the way down.

He hears their voices but can't make out what they're saying. They might be singing. Jesse, she says, can sing sweeter than any man you'll ever hear, sings the old hymns, and such blue eyes, deep and clear when he looks at you, makes you shiver. He once sat on Jesse's lap. He promises he won't forget to tell his children and she smiles and draws him close to her, where she is soft and warm. Eddy boy, my sweet Eddy, Mama loves you, she wishes she could have her little boy and her little girl with her all the time.

He thinks they have gone outside, even though it is dark. The voices sound far away, it might be the trees. There is no one to hear him going down the steps, opening the door. The moon makes long shadows on the porch and the air is warm, still.

And where might your mother be, boy? Mr. Starr carries a rifle in one hand, a string of birds in the other. Here, he says, look at this plump fellow. Some of the men stay a long time. She sits next to them on the porch steps. He can hear their voices from inside, but they do not talk loud. When he lies down in the high grass they can't see him. *Better lay low. Says he's going to get you.* The fiddler laughs and the birds sing.

He pulls the comb through his hair. Some day, she says, he will be a man, bigger than she is, tall as Mr. Starr. He doesn't want to be like Mr. Starr, his head shining through his hair, his hands with dark bristles growing all over the veins on top, his mustache thick and silvery, curling down over his lips. No, she says, she means *Sam* Starr, not old Tom. He'll be handsome like Tom's son Sam. The envelope is inside a small box in the drawer. He takes the hair out and brushes it across his cheeks, careful not to let any of it come loose from the yellow ribbon. His sister isn't here now. Pearl has been gone for some time, to Grandma Reed's, he thinks. His mother is gone too, but will come back soon. He watches the door.

The old men draw nearer. Several keep turning their heads to one side and spitting. The door will open and she will step out and see that he has stayed where she told him to. Look here, the man with the cane says, this is Belle's boy. You lost, boy? Some of the men are humming softly to themselves. This is Belle's boy sitting under a tree! The man points his cane at him, waving it in the air, then laughs. Belle's boy! Tell me, boy, do you know who's your daddy? Is it old Tom Starr? Huh? Look here, here's Belle's boy Eddy, sitting under a tree!

He can hear them up ahead. Their voices are soft, almost like whispers. Through the trees he can sometimes see her white dress, a sudden flash and then she is hidden again. The breeze is pleasant, warm, and the smell of the pine needles clean and strong. When she starts to climb the rocks she looks like a bird, perched there, the man behind her dark and knotted like shrubbery. At the mouth of the cave they stop and look down, but he is still and hidden by the shadows and the limbs of the trees and they cannot see him. The moon makes the rocks glow. The mouth of the cave is dark.

His daddy is named Jim Reed. He is gone away for a long time.

Would you like to come along, she asks. Sure, the man says, bring him along. He rides next to her in the buggy, not next to the man. The sky has a lot of color in it above the trees and the horse's tail swishes back and forth. When the men come late at night, he wakes up. They are on horseback. He can hear her moving about, her footsteps quick on the plank floor, and the horses neighing and stamping their hooves down below and the men saying things softly to one another. The floor makes his feet cold. From the window the men's hats look round as hoecakes. She steps out from the porch and mounts a horse that one of the men has brought for her, rising easily onto the side of the saddle, taking hold of the reins with one hand and with the other rubbing the neck of the horse.

In the buggy she lets him hold the reins. The horse doesn't mind and the man says, Eddy, you do that well. Then it is dark and she takes the reins. When you look up it is as though the trees are moving, going the other way down the road. Maybe she'd like to have these, Mr. Starr says, handing him the string of birds. Make mighty good eating. Tell her I give them to her. Some of Mr. Starr's teeth are black. The birds hang by their feet and their heads are shiny and smooth-looking. She will pull out all their feathers.

The place is all lit up with lamps and the people smiling and happy, talking loud and laughing. Let him sit up here with me, the man says, and she says, All right, sure, and they get him a chair. *Ain't he the cute one though! Going to dance with me, little feller?* The man takes the fiddle out of the case and strikes the strings, turning the pegs at the same time. Say, he says to the other man, show Eddy here your guitar. The other man has gray bristles all over his face and big hands with thick fingers. The guitar is heavy and has more strings on it than the fiddle. He doesn't want to play it, but the man says, Go ahead and hit it a lick, and so he does and the sound isn't pretty.

I like that fiddle, she says. I could listen to it all the time.

The explosion sounds like it is far away. The man sits down, and then he can't see him. Something has fallen. She comes out then, and even from down here he can hear her: Lord, Lord. What's happened! He runs, then stops quick, lies down flat against the damp ground. Someone else is running. He can hear the footsteps crashing down, a thumping noise, and the leaves hurt, sticks punch. He lies still.

I could listen to it all the time, she says. Some of the men she dances with he has never seen before, big men who swing her fast, making her skirt billow out so that you can see her ankles and her feet stepping quick, the heels of her shoes coming down hard on the floor. She smiles. The man plays the fiddle very fast now. *Two little sisters form a ring, now you're born, now you swing!* He listens to the footsteps. Someone is running fast, coming very close to him. Now he can see the figure. It is a man, walking towards him, no one he recognizes. He doesn't think it's

Mr. Starr. When Mr. Starr dances with her he stomps his heels loud and shouts. Her cheeks are red and sometimes her arms swing back and forth. *Going to dance with me, little feller?* The woman holds out her arms and he thinks that he will have to go with her but then she laughs and turns away and gets pulled by a big-bellied man into one of the circles of dancers and doesn't ask him again.

Are you the one killed that fiddler? Or was it your daddy did it? The old man leans on his cane, looking down on him, the others behind him humming softly but looking at him. He wants to run, but she has said he is to stay here until she comes back. He looks away from the old man, towards the door. Soon it will open. The old man is laughing.

The music makes him sad, but it is pleasant to listen to it. She has gone inside the cave and the fiddler stands outside, high above him, playing the tunes for her. Something bright flashes from time to time, something moving, maybe the silver tip of the bow. Yes, he thinks that is what it is. When he draws the bow across the strings, she says, My, ain't that fine. Do it again. And the man says, Here, press down your fingers like this. The sound is ugly. He wants to go to her but must lie still or else the man coming towards him through the brush will find him. He thinks maybe it is the fiddle that has fallen. *Now you're born, now you swing!* It's happy music. Everybody is having a good time. The fiddler's heel goes up and down when he plays, and he leans forward, his knees bent, the fiddle snug beneath his chin. Mr. Starr shouts. The old Cherokee man sits next to the lantern with his eyes closed, his cane resting across his lap.

He waits very still until he can't hear the footsteps anymore, then waits a little longer. He doesn't want them to find him. The ground is cold but he doesn't mind. When he looks up at the cave he can see her in her white dress. He thinks she is on her knees, but it is hard to be sure. It is probably the fiddle that has fallen. Maybe it has landed on a soft place. It's not heavy like the guitar, and the wood is thin and shiny and hard. When he tilts it something moves inside, something slides, but when he looks in through the narrow hole it is too dark to see anything. The man laughs. Snake rattle, he says. Put it in there to make the music better. From a big copperhead, the man says, biggest you ever seen. Killed him with a hoe. He was sidling right up to me like he didn't mean to stop. Saw that little tongue flickering and heard the tail rattling.

He thinks that might be where the magic comes from.

Reckon you lead a charmed life, she says.

He can hear the trees. He gets up slowly, looks around, can't see the man coming towards him anymore or hear the footsteps. The pistol still shines, but he has to be careful not to drop it and to keep the barrel clean. She holds it on her lap and rubs it with a soft cloth. Her necklaces are in a box that makes music when you open it up, and lined up neatly just beneath her bed are shoes and boots. The holster is in the big chest, laid down next to the pretty dress. She will wear the dress for him sometime, if he likes, but she thinks that it will probably not fit her the way it did then. That was before he was born.

Now he can run. The wind makes his face feel cool. He thinks that she is still up there with the fiddler, though he can't see her now, can see only the big rocks, the stars bright behind them, too many ever to count. In the buggy on the way home the man says, Ain't the stars beautiful, and she says, lovely, and the man has his hand on top of hers, the fingers curling around, but it doesn't look like he is squeezing hard. Just lovely, she says. In the daytime the sky is not as far away. When you go under the water and look up, the sky tries to follow you but it can't. It touches the water and makes the water shiver and turn white.

The rocks are smooth and cool. The fiddle may have fallen. He can't see it though. The old man has his eyes closed almost the whole time. Then, after the last dance, he opens them and lifts his cane, bringing it down hard on the floor and raising himself up. The door opens and there she is. Behind her a man in a dark coat holds onto her elbow and walks with her a little ways then stops, tips his hat, turns, goes back into the building. He can get up now, run and meet her, up the rocks, careful not to drop the pistol. If you look back you can see the space in the trees where the river is, and then, from a little higher, the river itself.

Eddy, oh Eddy, someone's killed him. The man lies still. She is bending over the man, holding his head in her arms. The man is holding onto the bow. She looks at the man and then at him. He doesn't want the pistol. Here, he says, handing it to her. She keeps it clean and shiny in the box. He always puts it back, but he can keep the shells. Someday she will teach him how to shoot it. He will be a man, bigger than she is, and when the land opens up he will have some of it of his own to build a house on and plant crops on. His life, she says, will be different from hers. He will tell his children that Jesse James was not a bad man, that the people who say so never knew him.

It's not Mr. Starr that comes towards him. He doesn't know who the man is, only that he steps quickly through the brush and comes near him and will find him if he looks. He must lie still. The man's legs are large and long though, like Mr. Starr's. In the water the sounds are far away, like singing, not one person singing, not her, but many voices. It might be the trees. When the fiddle plays, it sounds sad, not like at the dance. He can hear it fine down here. And see the man standing on the rocks outside the cave, playing the fiddle for her. There are many stars and the moon is full and bright, the dark edges of the trees all around against the bottom of the sky.

She is crying. He hands her the pistol, but she doesn't take it and so he puts it on a flat place where it will not fall off. He was a good man, she says. The man is still holding onto the bow, but the fiddle is not there. Where is it, she asks, where is his fiddle. He doesn't know. He thinks it has fallen off, but he hasn't seen it down there. Probably it is hidden in a good safe place. He shows her where he has put the pistol. She doesn't take it when she goes into town, but when the men come at night and wait for her on their horses she goes out and he sees that she has it strapped around her waist in the holster. She always brings it back.

Inside the cave it is very dark. He doesn't go far. When he turns around he can see her kneeling with the man's head in her lap. The light is bright out there. In here the rocks are smooth along the wall and the floor, and it is cool and quiet. You can walk deep into the mountain if you want to, but unless you're with someone who knows the way you might get lost. The fiddle is nowhere to be found. He thinks it might be hidden in the branches of the trees. Tomorrow, she says, we'll find it.

SAM STARR

The old man comes at him with a knife. Pa, he says, You put that down now. Somebody's like to get hurt. He decides not to wait and see, jumps out the window, head first. The breaking glass sounds like music, a lot of fiddles going lickety-split. He runs through the damp grass towards the trees and the path to the caves. When he looks back he sees that he is not being followed and therefore slows his pace, takes in the sweet green smells, the soft padding sound his steps make, the cool night breezes.

At it again, is he?

The voice comes from the trees. It's Belle, he knows. There is nothing to be afraid of. She walks beside him, her pistol secure in its holster. They come to the caves, and, once inside, it is as though they are in the dining room of a fancy hotel. He has the idea that this hotel is in St. Louis. The bright chandeliers hang from golden chains. All around hover tall, tightly jacketed waiters by the dozens, leaning like trees to provide shade from the hot light. Ain't this fine, she says. Didn't I say I'd take care of you? Trust Belle. He shivers. It seems to him that he has escaped nothing at all. The waiters will escort his father directly to this table, knives of their own drawn. Even now he sees, just outside the window, moving in a swift lope from one dark shrub to another, his father coming closer, eyes shining, fingers like fish.

It's no good, he tells Belle.

He gets up fast, runs.

It's not the same anymore. He remembers calling on Belle,

finding her on the porch with the fiddler. Why, Sam Starr! Ain't it a pleasure to see you! Riding across the Canadian, that shallow and red sandy-banked river, hardly a trickle this time of year, into the Choctaw Nation, down to the Fourche Maline, the swift and clear-flowing Kiamichi. Through the Moshulatubbee District and down to Tuskahoma, deep into the Apukshunnubbee, the wild country of the Winding Stair Mountains, roads giving way to paths and then to nothing at all. She finds the streams that flow down into the valleys, into the bottomland along the Muddy Boggy and the Red where the old settlers, Choctaws and their tenants, live in two-room cabins or frame houses among their cornfields, patches of green peas and sweet potatoes, cowpeas and beans. She waves at the families gathered to stare from the stoops and they wave back. So you're old Tom Starr's boy, she says. Well. Ain't I heard the stories about him! In Fort Smith they say, Rather meet the devil in the flesh than Tom Starr, that Cherokee killer. Say he once threw a baby into a burning cabin. And you his son!

In the camps she is quiet, sits off to herself away from the fire. Everybody knows not to bother her. She's thinking—not just laying plans, but thinking deep. On the trail she rides with Reed, until Reed gets shot down in Texas. Just you remember this, she says, what we are engaged in, me and you and the rest of the boys, is a business enterprise. It don't amount to more than that, and anyone says otherwise is a damn fool or a liar or both.

Don't she get a kick out of it though! He likes to watch her handle that long-barreled Colt navy. It's not just speed, not just accuracy, but it's passion too. He sees it in her eyes when she touches her palm to the butt of that pistol in its fine Spanish holster. He sees it in the way she sits in the saddle like it was a throne, her head held high, dark hair pulled back and held up on top with big silvery combs. What matters, she says, riding by his side beneath the broad blue sky, is how we live. Why we live.

There has to be reasons. Otherwise it's just a passel of lies, one after the other, every day, every breath a whiff of nothing.

Then the old man comes out of the trees. Sam, he says, you are my blood and don't you forget it. Blood's going to claim you. Ain't no escaping it. Next time *you* light the torches, *you* light the fires.

Giving up is Belle's idea. Go to Fort Smith, she says. Go before Parker's court. Otherwise it'll be the Cherokee tribunals. No mercy there, not for the son of old Tom! No mercy from Frank West, from Jim Middleton. No safety in the Choctaw Nation either, not for long anyway. Now, that's settled. Hitch up the buggy. Let's go to the dance!

Pearl steps up to him. He's rubbing down the mare, Belle's black Venus.

You ain't my daddy, she says.

He agrees with her, keeps rubbing—the hard flanks of the horse smooth and warm beneath his palms, the smell of hay and horse-sweat sweet in his nostrils but mixed now with the scent of Pearl, a woman-smell, breath of plumskin and peachfur. This is no little girl standing beside him, this is a woman, woman-child of his woman, his Belle's Canadian Lily, *Pearl*, her touch light and shivery like her mother's. He keeps his hands on that mare's haunches.

My daddy was a bad man, she says, name of Younger. He ran with Jesse James.

Where's your mama, he asks. You don't need to tell me nothing about your daddy.

Her hands are working at his shoulders as if at a lump of bread dough for her oven. Feels good. As he starts to fall, the horse's tail swishes his cheek.

Eddy's watching him. Eddy's in the shadows, leaning against the rocks. Up in the branches of the jackoaks. Down among the pine needles. Jim Reed's blood in him, strong and swift like the waters of the Mountain Fork. He remembers Eddy sitting on the porch off in the corner, the fiddle in his lap. Just a little boy, sent down from his Grandma Reed's in Missouri with his half-sister Pearl. Sits there stroking that fiddle like it was a cat curled up on his lap.

Where'd you get that fiddle, boy.
Found it. Mama said I could keep it.
Can you play it.
Reckon not.
Well, why'n't you try it?
Can't. Ain't no bow. Pearl broke it.
Easy to get you another one.
Don't want another.
Well, then, fix the broke one.
It's gone now.

It is cold. Belle is in the cabin, dancing. He can see the shadows of the dancers in the trees. It seems to him he has been here forever, clinging to the smooth trunk of this hickory, slipping downwards into a deep hole. At the bottom of the hole the old man waves him on, firing a Henry rifle into air that is thick like water, warm and slow-swirling. There is an explosion, but in the distance so that it cannot be considered a threat. Now he understands that the fiddle has stopped its singing. Across from him another man, sinking to the earth, calls out: Damn you, Sam Starr! Now Belle stands before him in her long dark dress and her white Stetson. She seems to have grown taller, and her eyes are set so deep in their sockets that they appear to be on the verge of disappearing. The wind has stilled, the air warmed. If he reaches out he will feel the cool rocks and know that he is safe in the caves. But there's no loosing himself from this tree. Let go and he falls.

Is he at it again? asks Belle.

Belle wants to make Eddy and Pearl genteel, decent and law-abiding citizens. Educated. Sit down here, Eddy, she says. You here, Pearl. I'm going to read you something just lovely. Sam, hand me that book. He knows without being told which book it is she wants. The Byron. A thick book with double columns, the brown leather cover worn at the corners. *So we'll go no more a-roving* . . . She reads standing up, holding the book in one hand and gesturing with the other. He likes the words, likes her performance, thinks her better than most actresses he has seen, even the ones in St. Louis, come out west all the way from the cities of the East and called the princesses of the modern stage. He sees Eddy frown, clench his fists, Pearl yawn. Belle keeps going, not even looking at the page now, her eyes closed, her gesturing hand still, held up in front of her as if it has found a hard place in the air to rest upon.

She lets her head drop as though in prayer, then looks up and closes the book. He sees the old man out the window. No, it is only the shadows, the lamp's glare. Eddy grins at him. Pearl winks. Belle again opens the book and begins to read.

But he's slipping now, feels himself going out of his skin and into the night. He's riding with his father, the old man leading the way, waving his snakeskin quirt in the air as though it were a saber. They ride at a furious gallop off into the thickets towards the trails that go deep into the wooded country of the Cherokees. Treaties, he says, I'll show them treaties.

He rides through a cornfield. It is late in the summer and the corn is high, but not high enough to provide complete cover. From the waist up he is exposed. He rides Belle's mare Venus, a fine horse that she dearly loves. The green corn smells fine. He remembers running, the stalks high above him on both sides, the husks plump and long, cornsilk dark and thick and curly like hair. The cornfields are the safe places. He can lie down in the rows between the high stalks where the ground is hard but cool, lie down on his back and watch the crows and the hawks fly across the portion of sky above him. He sleeps, stands high on a cliff overlooking a river. In the swift current of the river horses swim, not across but downstream, their great heads still, eyes unblinking, manes not wet at all but dry and flowing behind them. Beautiful, he thinks. A beautiful sight. They have learned that it is best to travel by water, not by land. Awake, he hears the hoofbeats. Galloping horses. These, he knows, will have riders. He puts the spurs to Venus, rides through the cornfield and into the thickets of black locust and persimmon trees. Soon he's to the canyon and still can hear the steady hoofbeats. It's cooler now, the horizon aglow, blue deepening into purple, the strong late afternoon wind here only a breeze pleasantly stinging his cheeks, a mist descending. At the river he clings to the trunk of a hickory sapling, feels himself sinking nonetheless, the horse, Belle's Venus, long gone, no use, shot out from under him and let float downstream.

He remembers the trees, how they sway darkly above, the stars beyond the leafy branches bright as the fires Belle tells him they really are. Those were summer nights, warm and windless, the air thick with quick-flashing lightning bugs. Belle's Colt navy shines in its holster and her horse moves beneath her with such easy grace that it might be a part of her self, a great hunk of her soul disguised as a horse. Jack Spaniard rides along behind, and

Blue Duck is there, and Childs, and John Middleton. Belle has pinned the brim of her white hat to one side and thereon placed a flurry of ostrich feathers that remind him of very white quick-moving fingers, her own gliding across the keyboard of the piano, playing a tune he's never heard before, fast and with a delicate lilt. The horses' hooves make a soft thumping sound on the trail and he is again living in those long nights with his father, searching out enemies, catching them unawares in their cabins. You either hunt, the old man says, or get hunted, kill or be killed. It is the law of life. It is the way we live.

Belle halts her horse with a gentle tug on the reins.

It's safe now, she says. Let's make camp.

Looky who's here, says Middleton.

If it ain't the Starr family, says Frank West. All of 'em out tonight.

Eddy stands in the corner, but she sees him right away. Didn't I tell that boy. Go take care of him, Sam.

He goes after Eddy, but the boy is fast and he can't catch him.

You're getting old, says Belle.

I'll take care of him later, he tells her, and then, looking hard at Frank West, adds, I got another score to settle just now.

The old man has gotten to Eddy and Pearl. He sees it in them sure as he remembers riding to Porum on the back of that horse, the broad slick haunches hard and warm, the trees along the road aquiver with darkness and music, back there behind them the bright fires burning the cornfields and consuming the cabins. *Come with me. Time you learned a thing or two.*

You've got to teach Eddy, Belle says. You've got to be a father to him now. He won't take nothing from me. I'll take care of Pearl. You take care of him.

Eddy sits beneath the tree with the fiddle on his lap, rubbing the back of it with a dirty piece of cloth from her scrap pile. Give me that, says Pearl. I want it. And Eddy, not but ten years old at this time, swings the bow at her, whacking her good with it, right across the side of her head. She doesn't blink an eye. He remembers thinking: She doesn't even feel it. She's so mad she doesn't even know she ought to be crying out in pain. And she grabs that bow away from Eddy, swift, swings it around above her head like it was a flag, then snaps it in two across her leg and tosses it back to him, surely before he can know what has happened, certainly before he can do anything to prevent it. Stomps off through the weeds, not running until she's sure Eddy's coming after her, and then he loses sight of them both, walks back towards the house hearing Eddy's shouts of anger, Pearl's screams of delight.

The moon has just risen above the top of the trees. By God, he loves this country. Loves it almost as much as he loves Belle, and for the same reasons—its rugged low-down beauty, its enfolding darknesses, its lawlessness, its soft furrows and sudden ravines.

Let's go dancing, Belle says. Hitch up the buggy.

It's December and cold. He remembers feeling a little dizzy, the swaying of the buggy getting to him, rocking him to sleep, Belle's voice low, soft, telling him a story, humming a tune. Then through the trees, as though *from* the trees, the sound of the fiddle, wild and sweet and so beautiful in its slippery notes and quick rhythms that he feels he might die happily at that moment. Here we are, says Belle. He sees the lights through the bare branches, can make out the shape of the cabin, its hard edges softened by the shadows. Something jumps out in front of the horses, and they rear back, leap, whinny. He is able to control them, but knows it might have easily been otherwise. Come on, says Belle. They've already started dancing. We missed the Grand Promenade.

Any minute now his father can come through the window, face painted like a Cheyenne's, eyes glowing.

Come on, Pearl says. You just relax and lie down here beside me. Ain't nothing to be afraid of. I'm tough as a wildcat. I'm strong as a bear. I got claws sharp as razors and long as Bowie knives. I'm telling you, Sam honey, she ain't no match for the likes of me!

He sees this: Belle—in a white nightgown, her long hair down over her bare shoulders—steps forward and raises one arm. She holds her rawhide quirt, aiming, he sees, to strike someone with it. The figure before her—in this light he can't tell if it's male or female—kneels, then crumples into a tight ball at her feet. She swings the quirt. It makes a sharp whacking sound, like a stick hitting a tree. The figure on the ground doesn't move, doesn't make a sound. She swings the quirt again. He thinks it might be Eddy that she whips. It might also be Pearl. It's too dark to tell. He turns, steps softly into the trees, then, on the path to the caves, runs as fast as he can.

He remembers how the fiddler leans forward as he plays. The faster the tune, the closer he seems to be to falling. He is a young man down from Briartown, his face smooth and pink, but his dark coat ragged and shining. How Belle does dance to that music! Her feet aflutter, her arms swinging like crazy, her dark eyes afire, she might be an angel for all he knows, brought to earth just for this night, not able to resist the sound of the fiddle coming up through the night sky, not the same woman who rides beside him and talks to Eddy and Pearl, tells him the old man is nothing to be afraid of and he should put all that out of his mind the same way you do a bad dream in the morning. She is the dream now, best he's had in a long time, dancing alongside him in the flesh, warm and high-spirited. His wife. His Belle.

He wakes hearing a noise in the next room, Belle's room. It is late in the morning, already warm, the sun shining through the south windows in broad dust-flecked beams. It surprises him that he has slept this time of day—a sign of age, he supposes. He hears the noise again, a drawer being pulled open, slowly, as though whoever is doing it wants to make as little sound as possible. He rises quietly, steps with stealth to the door, listens again. Nothing now. The wind in the trees. Has he only dreamed of hearing the sound? Belle is gone. He knows that for a fact, gone to Fort Smith and not likely to be back until the middle of next week. Her holiday. And Pearl is with her. He hears the sound again, this time pleased with himself for not thinking of his father except to conclude, *He is not here. He would not be here.* He opens the door just a crack, just enough to see. But all he sees is a beam of light across the big bed, making the white spread appear almost golden. Then a voice: *Don't come in here. Don't you come in here now.* He pushes open the door. The room seems vast, the light so brilliant that his first impulse is to shade his eyes. *I told you not to come in.* Eddy sits at Belle's dressing table, stark naked, his clothes in a little pile beside the chair. No one else seems to be in the room with him.

What the hell's going on here?

Nothing. Nothing's going on. I was looking for her pistol. She keeps it here in this drawer, I wanted to shoot it.

Eddy turns away from him, faces the mirror.

Get your clothes on, he says, and get out of here.

I got a right to be here.

No pistol's in there and you know it. She's got it with her.

Eddy answers without looking away from the mirror. Sits hunched over, his elbows on the marble top of the dresser.

I told you not to come in, he says, still looking in the mirror.

Belle walks at night, alone, through the woods, down by the river, climbs the rocks to the caves. He goes with her sometimes, but not so much lately. She sits up there, just inside the mouth of the cave, and stares straight ahead, not seeing him, he's sure, probably not seeing anything there, stars in the night sky pretty as they can be, big rocks washed white by the fierce moonlight beautiful to behold. It may be that she's there now, listening hard for the sound of that ghost fiddle. *You listen too, Sam. You can hear it if you listen.* Or it may be that she's outside looking in. She's quiet. Quiet and swift.

You afraid of my mama?

Pearl leans down and whispers it in his ear. You got nothing to be afraid of. She's scared to death of you. We all are. You're a big tough hombre, Sam Starr.

Belle doesn't love him anymore. He knows it from the way she dances with the young men. She favors a young Creek named Jim July. Of course he knows about the Cherokee Blue Duck, and there was that betrayer John Middleton, but in those days it doesn't matter. She makes him know he's the one she loves. He feels it even before Jim Reed's death down in Texas. She sees someone she takes a liking to, she goes after that fellow. Down in Tuskahoma an old Choctaw steps up to him and says, You Sam Starr. One thing I want to know and you're the one can tell me. What I want to know is: Is it true what everybody says that Belle Starr sleeps in the same bed with that sixteen-year-old son of hers?

No. That's not true.
Ain't it now.
No. Get out of my way.
Surely.
The old Choctaw tips his army-issue hat and saunters around him as though dancing.

After all what does it mean to love, to be loved. He thinks of Pearl touching him while he rubs down Venus. He sees Belle as she is on that first day, up from Texas with Jim Reed, that smile, those dark eyes. He is on the scout, riding in order to hide from those that hunt him, passing the familiar camps, the smooth clearings in the willow brakes, in the blackjack thickets, in the pines, the caves. He is desperate. He has always been desperate, but breathes easier in those spaces. What has he done other than fight to stay alive? Do what has to be done? Belle laughs. What does she find so amusing? It's you, Pearl tells him. You so solemn all the time with your talk of love, like you was a preacher. Eddy crouches by the fire, holding the fiddle towards it as though to warm it. I might play it, he says, if I wanted to. The fiddle's back glows red, flashes this red across the clearing to where he, Sam Starr, clings to the hickory sapling, so smooth its bark that he cannot get a proper grip on it and so continues to slip downwards. Desperate, he shouts for help. To his surprise, he realizes he has called out his father's name. Pa, he says, I ain't done nothing. The old man, drawing the Bowie knife, says, That is the truth, Son. And comes at him.

JIM JULY STARR

Better come quick, Pearl's telegram says, my mama's shot dead. He rides hard. Damn right. It's February, the wind stiff but clean and the sky gray and smooth like cat fur. By nightfall Watson's face seems to stare at him, mean and sunk-cheeked, caught in the spindly branches ahead of him and to all sides of him, shimmery, slivers of moon shining from a lot of dark ponds. A man like that on the loose, this is no time to turn yourself in. Got to ride west fast and hard, back into the Choctaw Nation, across the Poteau and the San Bois and the hard-humped hills in between.

Well, says Watson, and what is it like in those parts.

Belle just grins. Like hell, she says, only a little better. Stroking the nose of her mare, she smiles, looks into the horse's eyes. Watson is laughing, damn his soul. Reckon he's come to the right place, he says.

Be sure, Belle says, you show Mr. Watson the way out, Jim.

Jim, something about that man I don't like. You notice the way he looked at me, up and down, like he was inspecting a piece of horseflesh?

I get lonesome, Jim. That's all. This is lonesome country. I'm not an ornery person at heart. My disposition is warm. I want to trust.

There are plenty, he supposes, besides Watson that she hadn't ought to trust. Her own daughter, for example. Clear up in Catoosa, way down in Tuskahoma, they talk about Pearl. Pearl sidles up to him and touches his cheek, says, Jim, how come you treat me like I'm a little girl when here I am a growed-up woman. I got charms my mama never even dreamed of.

And her own son Eddy says, Jim, tell her I'm gone to the meeting house over to Eufaula. Rides off on her mare and stays gone for days, comes back pale, his eyes ringed dark as though the nights have rubbed off on him, nights he's spent in God knows what hell-hole with what companions and what rotgut whisky. It's the horse she minds most. Loves that horse and won't have anyone, son or not, abusing it who is better than any human being she ever come across. He watches her take hold of Eddy, grab his arm and pull him off to the barn, Eddy with his head bowed down, his lanky body going limp, long feet kicking up the dust but half heartedly, no fight in him, that's for sure.

Who can she trust? *Him*, that's who. Jim July. Jim July Starr. Her Jim. He calls himself Starr not because he wants the right to her improvements, no, but because it is her name. Middleton grins. Maybe, he says, old Tom's gonna have something to say about that. You know old Tom Starr, Jim, don't you? Hell, yes, he knows Tom. Don't nobody *not* know him in these parts. This is a matter, Jim says, between Belle and me. Ain't none of Tom Starr's business. And Belle asks:

What are you, Jim July?

A man, he tells her, just a man.

I can sure enough see that, she says. But what kind of man. That's what she wants to know, and so he says Creek, I am of the Creek Nation, the descendant of chiefs, of warriors in the olden times before the Great Removal from Georgia and Alabama. He don't remember none of that, no, but has heard the stories so many times that he feels it all might as well have happened to him and so it is a part of what he is, isn't it. And you want to turn things back, she asks, go back to the old ways? He's got to laugh. No use, he says. No use to hope for that.

What then. What is it any use to hope for?

Nothing. You just got to take what you can get.

Spoke like a horse thief.

She smiles, her lips tightening but not parting, the little lines in her cheeks going deep, dark and many branched like rivers, as sweet to see. The face shines before him as he rides, lost, the line of mourners filing past her plain coffin, the old Cherokees dropping pieces of cornbread into it. Watson stands alongside Pearl and Eddy. Tom Starr, tall and grizzled, his boots caked with red mud, leans against the doorframe of the cabin, spits in the dirt. She was one of us, Tom says. We thought of her as like one of us, from the first time she come into the Nations. You was just a little boy in them days, Jim July. I'd atook her for myself but my boy Sam beat me to it.

He's lost. She's led him out here and left him. Where's his whisky. There. Goes down hard, deep and warm. Good corn liquor from Catoosa. None of that coalcamp Choc beer.

What trail is this. Ain't the Whisky Trail, ain't any trail he can remember riding with Belle. River's too broad for the Canadian, too silvery and smooth, too deep and too quiet. Is it the Kiamichi, the Fourche Maline? Has he come so far south? It would be the Choctaw Nation. They got no love for him down here. He keeps to the trees, looks for the moon, which way west.

Walking in the woods near the caves, he comes to a bright clearing and stops to rest. It's still early spring, but warm in the sunshine, the patch of sky above him cloudless and deep blue, the weeds beneath him stiff and dry, pressing up against his shoulder blades like hard little pine needles. Birds rise from the treetops, bunched together in a swarm, dark and swift, all atwitter. He closes his eyes, breathes in the clean air. Belle stands before him, legs spread apart, clenched fists pressed against her hips.

She is older than he remembers her, streaks of gray in the dark shiny hair, a trace of a mustache above her thin lips, and he has the feeling that he has done something wrong. She will punish him, snatch a willow switch and lash him with it. Eddy, crouching next to him, smells of horse sweat, a thick and dank scent strong enough, it seems like, to bite into. She gets like this sometimes, Eddy says, whispering, the breath warm in Jim's ear. Now you'll know how I feel. And Belle says, Come here, Eddy. But Eddy's run off into the jackoak thickets. *Come here right now. Will you stand there and disobey your mama?* She's staring straight at him, her Jim July Starr, and he sees that she means business. He turns tail and lights out after Eddy, but Eddy's long gone, nowhere in sight. There's no trail and white light flickers through the lip-shape leaves and the black trunks of the trees.

The ground is hard and cool. He presses his cheek against it, tastes the dust. *She's down there now!* Where is he. He rises, sees that it's morning. Already the sun is up over the treeline. Come on, his father says. If you mean to go with us, step brisk now. Here. Grab hold. I'll help you up. But he reaches for the sides of the wagon, stepping up on the wheel spokes, and it hurts. He mustn't tell them, mustn't let on. Only splinters. He'll suck the slivers out later when no one's watching, when they're in the store. But that's when *she* comes, comes walking out of that little shack of a store with a tall dust-coated man by her side, walks straight towards the wagon as if she's had it in mind all along, knows exactly what she wants from it, knows he's there sucking at the splinters in his thumb and watching her, already loving her. Wouldn't I like me a little man like that, she says, and the man laughs, says, Sure, that's what you need, Belle, just what you need. The man leans down towards him and squeezes his arm like he was testing a piece of fruit he might pick for the lady if it was ripe enough. The lady says, Keep your hands off of him, Sam, and pulls the man away. He watches the two of them mount dark stallions, hers a roan, he remembers it well, with a thick black mane and broad rippling haunches. They ride away and don't look back.

He rises. He's Jim July Starr. A man. It's 1889. Belle's dead, gunned down while she rides back to Younger's Bend. This much he knows. It's not enough. The bare trees shake their limbs at him, the wind so strong and cold he thinks of the grave, longs for it. It will be warm in its way and there will be no wind.

He's got to figure things out. *What are you, Jim July.* Hell, he's of the Creek persuasion, that's what he's always said, a Creek unredeemed and proud of it. That's been enough. But wait, slow down now, no use hurrying back just for a funeral. Here's Belle —that's the beginning—walking up to him who is going on thirteen years old even if he appears to be no more than ten, looking down on him in the wagon as though at a baby in a cradle. What next. Them stories. The low voices of the old men. His father and grandfather and the uncles, gathered together evenings in the cabin, lined up in front of the big black stove as if talking to it instead of to each other. They talk of the old places, of Sawanogee, Woccocau, Mooklausa, of Red Eagle and the treacherous Jacksa Chula Harjo, of the Great Removal, the land left behind, the slaves, the handsome horses. Ain't no justice in this world, they agree.

The wind is cold now, the sky full of fast-shifting clouds, ragged and dark, low enough to scrape across the top branches of the trees. He slows his horse to a walk. How much farther? He can't say for sure. He feels like he's always been in these woods, everywhere. There before him stands the cabin at Briartown. Again the sky is black and the cabin is bright with lamps. He hears voices, many people talking at once. A fiddle's playing. Now Sam Starr steps quick out the door of the cabin. *Come and get me*, he says. The other man fires first. The fiddle stops playing. Sam hangs onto the trunk of a hickory sapling. He looks like he's hugging it, but you can tell he's slipping fast and'll soon be on the ground in a clump and looking just like the other man, blood mixing with dirt that is so red it might have been bled into every season of its life. A cricket is chirping, but then the screams start up and Belle is kneeling at Sam's side, shutting his eyes, saying to the fiddler, who leans over her shoulder like he means to catch poor Sam's soul before it gets away, You hadn't ought to stop playing, A.B. Get back in there and play that fiddle and don't stop unless it catches fire on you. Here, she says. You there, Jim July. Help me move this man. He does as she says. He is strong. He is twenty-one years old, a man. He moves quick, knows it, feels her eyes on him as he puts his arm around the body of Sam Starr, lifts, pulls it away from the little tree, the bootheels dragging across the hard ground, and brings it to rest right where he has pointed to, a grassy moonlit patch not more than ten yards from where it fell. Belle takes the scarf from her neck, folds it carefully, places it beneath Sam Starr's head, then goes back in the cabin and dances. Dances all night to that fiddle.

You can still hear it, you listen hard. No, not all the time. Of course not. Night of the Harvest Moon. Listen. You'll hear a fiddle if you listen hard.

His father laughs, but the grandfather goes on, no trace of a smile on *that* old face, the chin grooved and slated so regular it might be taken for a pine cone, eyes gone back so deep you think they are hiding out, waiting for the right time to ambush you.

Could be it's just A.B. playing.

No. It ain't A.B. A.B's still alive.

Sure, his father says. How else is that fiddle going to get a bow drawed acrost its strings. I ask you that.

Listen. I'm telling you. This is the other fiddler. The killed one from long ago. The one killed at the mouth of the cave. The one shot down while he played the fiddle for Belle. He's still playing for her, you see. Only you can't hear him all the time.

Just on the night of the Harvest Moon.

That's right.

Who was this fiddler, that's what Jim wants to know. She loved him, that's all anyone remembers. That and the fact that he was one damn fine fiddler. Had the sweetest touch you ever heard. Was shot down while playing the fiddle for her who was inside the cave, listening. Who shot him? Nobody can say. Weren't no arrest made. Someone wanted that fiddler dead. A rival. A lover. An outlaw.

When did this happen.

Long ago.

Everything happens long ago. Listen to these stories long enough and you think you've lived about a minute. How old is Belle. Old enough, she says, smiling, to know some things you don't know. Come here close. I'll show you what the old folks know. Everybody's heard of Belle. She's in the stories. Is there really a Younger's Bend? Sure, there certainly is, says the old man. Not a long ride from here either. At the edge of the Cherokee Nation, on the Canadian River. That's the place where she lives. I been there. I seen the bluffs, the cliffs, the mouths of the caves. Belle walking the paths down by the Canadian, the plumes in her broad-brimmed hat a-dancing in the wind, Cole Younger with her, a big man, hefty and tall, keeping just a step or two behind her. When was that. Oh, long ago, before you was even able to walk. More Youngers than anybody needed in them days. James Boys too. I seen them all, Jesse with his blinking blue eyes, and mean Jim Reed that gets her with Eddy and then gets himself killed down Texas. Nobody knows where they been when they come here. They just show up, slick and grinning. They know Tom Starr. And Tom Starr is here first, brought to the land of the Western Cherokee by a daddy who is later shot in bed by the henchmen of Chief John Ross, and that is why old Tom and his brothers and later his sons take to killing and, some say, thieving. Out of vengeance.

But he knows better. Walking those woods he knows the desire for revenge don't count for much. No, it is something more than that, as though breathed into your bloodstream like a germ. Land, Belle says. It's all a fighting for dirt. You're never going to figure it out, honey. *It's a lusting after dust*.

You'd think enough of it got breathed in to satisfy most anyone.

And Pearl says: I had a dream she was dead in the dirt.

Hush, says Eddy. Dreams don't mean a thing.

Why do I got to hush then?

Just hush up. I don't want to hear your dreams.

Maybe Jim does. Jim, you want to hear my dream?

Pearl's hands are tiny, the fingers like little stubs but the nails long and tapering. She smells of the insides of houses, like a warm room with the windows steamed over. Maybe it is a hotel room. He can't see Belle in her face. Belle's face is lean, firm of jaw and cheek, skin drawn taut over bones that seem all corners, her mouth as if carved from wood, good hardwood, hickory. Pearl's is a baby's face that nobody has ever said no to. Round. Pink. Cheeks like silk. The spitting image, Belle says, of her daddy. Does she mean of Cole Younger? Belle smiles then, a quick grin, and pulls him close. Don't you worry about Cole Younger, she says. He's up north in a prison.

One night Tom Starr walks up to him, says, Follow me. Belle, sitting in a high-back rocker, aims her pistol at a tree, fires. He sees that Eddy is up in the branches of that tree, shooting back at

Belle with a shotgun. Tom Starr leads him into the forest. They come to a burning cabin. That's it, says Tom. Go on, look in that window there, see what you see. He sees his father, his grandfather, all the old men, sitting all in a row, just like always, their black vests shining, in front of the big woodstove, only with flames jumping up all around them. If we'd been a little sooner, Tom says, we mighta saved them. That's what comes of tarrying.

Tell him what it means.

Watson laughs. He never had a dream in his life. Never dreams, no sir, just sleeps, sleeps and wakes. Sleeps good, wakes rested. There he sits, slouched down in the chair that Belle says was Jim Reed's favorite, a high-back chair with low squat legs carved on the ends to look like bear claws. Belle turns, strikes a chord on the piano, sings:

> *It was a dream, a warning dream*
> *That heaven sent to me*
> *To snatch me from a drunkard's doom*
> *Grim want and misery.*

Mighty pretty, says Watson. You sing like a bird, Belle. A nightingale.

Watson is new in the Territory, but Belle says she don't hold that against him. A man wants to get ahead in the world, why he strikes out for new parts. A clean slate.

Tell that to a Indian, says Watson.

I'm staying put, says Eddy. I'm staying right here.

I'm going a long ways away, says Pearl. Going to take Jim here along with me.

I'm staying home with Mama, says Eddy. Somebody's got to.

Old Oklahoma's going to be opened up soon, says Belle. If I was a man I'd be thinking about staking me a claim. I'm thinking about it anyway.

I seen that country, says Watson. A feller'd starve for sure on one of *them* claims.

What does that man know, who never dreams.

I dream, says Belle, I'm back in Missouri. My daddy is laying out beneath a big tree, maybe it is a maple, and I'm watching him from the porch. It's the old homeplace back in Jasper County, Missouri. I know this even though the tree is one I don't recognize, and the porch is bigger than any I ever saw. Something shines and flashes in that tree. I don't know what it is, but I know it's dangerous and so light out for the tree, Daddy asleep and not able to see what's hanging there above him, ready to fall or leap. Such a long ways to run! I hadn't thought it was so far when I started out. There is a river to get across. Daddy's awake now, shouting for me to hurry up. Mama's at the riverbank, all dressed up, leaning forward ever so little on a parasol. I see that she is having her picture made, and then the picture-taker steps out from under the drapes of his big camera and I see that he is Daddy. Mirrors, he says to me. It's mirrors.

Belle, says Jim July, this trail leads everywhere. Out to the west the earth is flat as a floor but cracked and split up in places as if the hills and rises have been dropped down deep somewhere in a trap. Out there the wild Cheyenne, living in tipis and starving for want of buffalo meat, keep to the old ways. It was trouble at first, the grandfathers say. The Creek has forgotten how to protect himself. The Osage must think we are white. We build our cabins like whites, cultivate our fields like whites, then get raided like the whites. It has been a long time since we are fighting with Red Eagle and Tecumtha against Jacksa Chula Harjo. The Creek are to the Cheyenne and the Osage what the white Georgians and Alabamans are in the old days to the Creek. I see this now. I do not know where all this will lead, says Grandfather, what it all means.

When the piano is hauled in, Belle says, Now these trees are going to sing, jackrabbits dance. He listens hard, he watches, but all is quiet, nothing moving. He is very tired. He would like to close his eyes, but when he does he sees more than he wants to. Belle in the woods with Watson. Tom Starr, torch in hand, stalking the killers of his father, his boys gathered behind him, eyes agleaming. Eddy climbing onto Belle's mare Venus, stroking her neck, whispering in her ear. Pearl lying spreadeagle on the big featherbed, smiling at him. Jim July, she says, why you so afraid of me. A big man like you. Hush. What if your mama was to — She's clear over to Fort Smith, buying herself a new hat. And there's Sam Starr, still holding onto that hickory sapling, inching downwards real slow, light from the bonfire making his face look white like a lady's. Pa! Sam shouts. Where's Pa? As if that old man would help any.

Sees the line of mourners filing past the open casket, the old Cherokees hunched over, pieces of cornbread in their dark and knobbed fists. Even the dead, they say, have got to eat.

The hell you say.

What are you, Jim July?

Lost. Soon's he gets the telegram he rides out of Fort Smith, Judge Parker be damned, he's innocent anyway, and this is important isn't it. That was a while back. He remembers the flask. Two of them in fact, fit nice and snug in the saddlebags, and a third in his hand. He's wanted to ask her, these many months now, these two, these three years since Sam Starr's death that he has been Jim July Starr, what happened that time up in the caves with the fiddler. The others she's loved—Cole Younger, Jim Reed, Middleton, Blue Duck, Sam Starr, even Watson if Watson is one of them—don't matter. But this fiddler now, the one they say is shot down at the mouth of the big cave, he's the one the grandfathers talk about.

You believe in ghosts, he asks Eddy one time.

Hell fire, says Eddy, I *am* a ghost.

Watson laughs: Bet I could prove you wasn't.

Pearl, spreadeagle on the bed, reaches down and touches herself, smiles at him, says: Come here now, Jim July. Put that old woman out of your mind. She'll die on you before you know it and you and me got our whole life ahead of us.

Die? What does she mean by that.

Why, nothing, honey. Just that she's older than you and me. That's all. Most likely she'll die before we do. I didn't mean nothing else by it. Now come here.

Die! She's not dead. Hell, no, not Belle.

What the hell's the matter with you anyway! Ain't I old enough for you?

What life is left. Our whole life. Shit. He listens hard. He's got to be close to the caves by now. It's all back there, that's where the place is, in the fiddler's tune. If only he could hear it. It's the wrong time of year, sure, but ain't he on the right track. Look at that moon! Like a saucer. Bright? Let me tell you—and them trees leaning west, like they was pointing the way.

EDDY THE MAN

Her quill pen in hand, her mirror before him, he means to set down an account of what has happened. *My dear beloved mother has been shot down and killed. Having attained the year of my majority, yet have I witnessed much that makes me wise beyond my years.* Oh, that is a lie, a barefaced lie. Her boy Eddy, that's all he is. Rising, he throws the quill to the floor. Help him, Mama. He's in trouble, bad trouble. Outside, the sky opens up and the trees lean in the direction of the fleeing clouds. He remembers her stepping towards him, the quirt upraised, and he wants to tell her he loves her, she mustn't be mean to him, sometimes he's not himself, he's no one at all. Her face is in his, her thoughts are inside his head, inside *that* head, he would as soon not claim it, that chin with the coarse hairs curling, that nose with its openings so delicate and small that you wonder how it ever lets in air enough, that mouth like a cut place healed wrong. Tears come, he can't never seem to stop the tears, anything will set tears to flow from them eyes she looks out of with him, anything looked at long enough, a mane, a creekbed, a face, anyone's face, even Pearl's his sister's his mama's Canadian Lily's face with its smug smile and pink cheeks and lips like slabstone. We are of different fathers, he thinks at the burial of his mother, and that has made all the difference, that and the fact of gender, Pearl's womanhood coming on her like drunkenness at about the age of nine, never once letting up. She stands by his side like a wife, holding hard to his arm. One by one the mourners shuffle past the open coffin, Starrs and Vanns and Riders and Lynches and Mayfields, the old ones with the crusts of cornbread crumbled in their palms. *Cry now if you are going to cry. It won't be manly later. Weep when the rest of them weep.* No one weeps.

The last bits of cornbread are no sooner dropped into the coffin than Jim July, his mama's last love, a man not much older than himself, maybe twenty-five, with his hair flowing down to his shoulders like a wild Cheyenne instead of the long-tamed Creek that he is, steps forward and says, Arrest this man, pointing his long finger at Watson, and Watson laughs, his teeth small in a small mouth, rounded at the edges and unnatural white. He always looks like a man that has just come from a fight. Eddy expects Watson to dive for Jim July, forget pistol or knife and simply bite into July's leg with his small white teeth, but no, Watson is the soul of decorum. You have the wrong man, Watson tells Jim July. I am innocent of this outrage. I am no more guilty than you, than Eddy, than Pearl.

I remember her wedding day, Pearl says later. Do you, Eddy?

He does.

We was just children, but I can remember it as clear as—why, it might have just happened. And there she is, in her coffin.

She speaks as though she is looking at that coffin, but they ride along the banks of the Canadian, Jim July not far behind with Watson. It is a cloudless day. It is February. However there has been a warming and no snow all winter to speak of. Rain. Sleet. The road's muddy.

My, wasn't there a lot of men in Mama's life! Oh, don't frown so. It is nothing to be ashamed of. I mean to have plenty in mine too. It is my nature.

Already had plenty. Made one a father.

What of it. It is what we're here for, the way I see it.

Maybe there is another reason, but he won't answer her. What is the use. What else is there anyway. At the wedding Sam Starr has his boots polished, same boots he dies in six years later, the boots pretty dull then, soles worn thin as leaves. Sam curls around the trunk of a hickory sapling, no telling how many bullets in him. Sam, she always says, you ain't much of a daddy. As much as my own was to me, Sam says. And yet, hanging onto that sapling, Sam cries out for his daddy. Pearl has forgotten that. Fathers, she tells him, don't count. Not, he supposes, for the likes of us, horse-thieves at heart, yearning in our blood for what don't belong to us, what no one ought rightly to have.

When Pearl stops talking, he hears the water in the river, the wind in the trees, the leafless branches rubbing against one another, the low murmuring of Jim July and Watson, the breathing of the horses, and the soft plop of the hooves in the puddled trail. The wind is strong, always is, but not so cold yet, the sun just gone down, something of March in that wind. He can't make out the words of July and Watson, but the tone is not of anger. Occasionally July, probably passing the flask to Watson, laughs in his low-pitched, soft-spoken way. We'll take him in, July says that morning. We'll get him to Fort Smith and see what Judge Parker has to say about all this.

How will we get him to come along peaceably, he wonders.

We'll persuade him somehow.

Sure, says Pearl. I know how you will persuade him.

Think you can do better, honey.

Damn right.

We will call on you if we need you.

They don't need her. They ride up to Watson's, find him sitting on that little front porch he has made *to provide shade for leisure times:* sitting there in a fine new rocker, the wind whipping his face with his own hair, the thin hanks of it that border his bald pate like old fringe snapping across his cheeks. With a long Bowie knife, he whittles on a stick as big around as a wrist.

Wouldn't call this porch-setting weather, says July.

Good enough for me, says Watson, grinning like he was showing off his little white teeth.

Me and Eddy here come to take you in.

That right. All by yourself.

Watson keeps his eye on the stick, the knife not missing a lick, the shavings falling at his feet and then blowing away, and you get the idea that he is amused with hisself, that there is possibly some joke between him and the stick. The front door opens and Watson's wife Mandy pokes her head out. She has got black hair pulled tight against the sides of her head and clamped firm in back, and her face is so narrow and hard-looking it might be all chin, the rest stuck on.

I got coffee hot if anybody is a mind to drinking it, she says.

July slides down from his horse. Eddy does the same, and Watson drops the piece of wood, jabs the knife into the arm of the rocker, and leads them into the front room of the cabin, which is bright and cheery and warm and smells of dry wood burning and strong coffee and lye.

Hardly anybody come to see us anymore, Watson's Mandy says, pouring the steaming coffee. Ain't that right, Bob. We get downright lonesome, sitting here by ourself.

That is a fact, says Watson.

We was so sorry to hear of your misfortune, but ain't it consoling how grief brings folks together. It just makes me more certain than ever that Belle Starr was a good woman, at heart.

He sleeps in her bed, like always when she is away, ever since he can remember. She tells him it is all right. Sometimes she calls for him, her voice faraway as though in a dream, then a whisper that is no dream, her hair brushing his cheeks. *Come keep Mama company.* Sam's gone on the scout, and Sam's not his daddy anyway. His daddy is dead, buried in Texas. He has seen the stone and has leaned flowers up against it, a long time ago, when the fiddler comes and takes her for walks along the river where it is hard to follow them. Pearl's summer clothes, the pale-colored calico smocks and gingham pinafores she doesn't need up at Grandma Reed's in Missouri, lie neatly folded under the bed, wrapped in old newspapers, the *Cherokee Advocate*, the *Fort Smith Elevator*, shut tight in a canvas traveling bag. Mama gets lonesome, she tells him, her hair swishing across his cheeks. She can talk to you and tell you things she wouldn't never tell nobody else. Not even Pearl? Not even Pearl. Pearl can talk just fine, but she don't listen. You listen.

He remembers, drawing the silk pallet up around his shoulders, taking up the pen again, that low voice, the sweet warm breath, the moon chasing shadows on the ceiling, that stillness strange as trees. Where in hell is he. In the very center of the world, it seems like. Younger's Bend, I.T. The names of other places are surely pitiful names in comparison with this one. No one will never find us here. We will always keep this place secret.

On the other side of the room, Pearl, curled up in a blanket, breathes deep from her sleep. She will be ready when the time comes. Mounted on her Indian pony that is almost pink, almost the color of her own skin, she will say, Let's go, boys. Let's get that son of a bitch in jail where he belongs. In the summer Eddy walks with her down by the bluffs, along the path that comes to the river, the sky always breaking through the trees, the wind stiff and hot. Almost a head taller than he is, she takes hold of his hand as though she considers him still a baby, not the boy of eleven he is then, that youth capable of firing pistol or rifle and riding long distances without hardly tiring. He pulls loose, running, and comes to the sun-warm rocks by the river, lies down and listens to the beat of her footsteps, the branches snapping, the water awash over the rocks. *Eddy! You devil you, I'll get you, I'll show you a thing or two!* He sticks his hand in the water, so shallow here that he can feel the smooth pebbles—fish eggs, Pearl calls them—tiny and cool against his palm. He lets his fingers dig into the sandy bottom. Then she is on top of him, straddling him, her black boots crossed beneath him like smooth mossy branches. *Giddyup, damn you!* Standing, he tries to throw her off, but she is heavy and strong and won't let loose, her thick skirt finally tripping him. On the ground she squeezes hard, one arm around his neck, the other across his shoulders, and they roll into the water, he can't tell if she is shrieking with fear or anger or pleasure.

Pleasure. For sure, because she is laughing, sitting next to him with her legs spread out, the wet skirt clinging, shiny as satin with the creek water. *I am a woman now. Mama says so. Are you a man now?* How is he supposed to know. Will there be a sign, will something happen to him that will tell him now he is a man, his boyhood over.

Yes, he says. Sure. I am a man.

How do you know?

Same way you know you are a woman.

Do not! Mama says it is just for girls.

I can ride. I can shoot.

So can any five-year-old with a lick of sense. Boy *or* girl!

He listens and watches in his mama's room, hears his mama's voice and sees her lips form sounds that won't quite be words. When he moves his head, scarce enough to make the pillow stir, the mirror flashes back a faint circle of light. Pearl is whispering, You tell me your secrets, and I'll tell you mine.

They ride all night. July and Pearl are just visible ahead, Pearl's hat tiny as a thumbnail, the trees alongside them close and thick.

Eddy rides with Watson, who sleeps erect in the saddle, his head leaning only a little to one side. Surely soon the sky will lighten, stars dim. It has been a calm, cold night, little wind, the sky starry, frost gleaming on the open meadows and the rooftops of the dark cabins in the clearings. To keep from weeping, he watches his gloved hands, or Watson, or the ground. A boy, he follows at a distance, kneels quick behind a bush if his mama and the fiddler pause or seem about to turn. When they stop, he climbs a jack oak. He can see them just fine then. Most of the other men he has been introduced to before, in Eufaula or Tuskahoma, lanky men smelling of dust even in their dark frockcoats and high-crowned hats, their sideburns curled. He can place them by gait and gesture as Cherokee or Choctaw, by breadth of brow and tilt of nose as intermarried or pure. He can't place the fiddler at all. The old Cherokee men up in Tahlequah come up and ask the fiddler's name, leaning down as though they might fall if he doesn't answer quick, clutching his shoulder, patting his head, shaking his hand. *You are Belle's boy. You ought to know!* They spit in the dirt, walk toward the trees.

Listen, says Watson, I'm going to tell you who killed your mama. It wasn't me. Now listen. Are you listening to me? Listen close. It was Jim July. I seen him. I was watching from back of the trees. He is the one that done it. Belle, he calls out, Belle, and she looks right at him and he pulls the trigger. That's the way it happened. Lord help me if it ain't the truth.

Lord help him then. July is in Fort Smith at the time, everybody knows that, and it is Watson's shotgun that has been found in the bushes near the spot where, face down in the mud, she falls.

I come from Arkansas, Watson says. Yell County, near Blue Mountain. He doesn't climb down from the wagon, which has never really stopped, just slowed down long enough for him to shout his name, Bob Watson, and where he is from. His wife, her long face without expression, sits stiff by his side and looks towards the river.

If he is from Yell County, Mama says, then I am from Paris, France.

Over in Fort Smith, July says, they say he comes from Florida, a white slaver.

I think, Pearl says, he is a handsome man.

Handsome! Have you seen him grin.

It's them eyes. He don't have to grin, eyes such as that.

Better not let Mama hear you talk like that.

She ain't running my life.

True enough, he thinks, but she is financing it, already paid for one bastard, probably paid off the father too, in which case she has had to pay two or three, maybe more claimants, for Pearl has wasted no time. *It is what we are here for.* Breathing heavy now, on the other side of the room, she starts to whisper. *Yes, yes,* and the crickets go crazy up in the blackjacks, moonlight so bright in the room that he can see all he wants to in the rosewood-framed mirror above his mother's dresser, his face already a ghost, hers, his own eyes looking at him as if to say, Who are you, what are you, and where. *I'm listening, Mama.* But what is there to hear, save your Canadian Lily and the crickets and the hoofbeats and soon the birds starting up again. Is that all I am supposed to hear. Alone, riding to Catoosa on her black mare Venus, he hears her tell him that he has got to stay out of trouble because this territory is going to change and then a man can make something new and fine out of his life. It is going to happen fast when it happens, she feels it coming soon now, and he better get ready. He rides hard to Catoosa that time. What is it, he asks, going from saloon to saloon, what in the hell is it that I have got to get ready for, boys, that is going to change everything, make it so fine and new. What makes her think she knows so much. Nothing is going to happen, he is going to sit here in this saloon and listen to the bootheels drag across the plank floor, cards slap down on the tabletops, the voices come together as if through a funnel into the top of his head. From now on, that is the way it will be. Pass him that corn likker. Belle's boy. Hell, ain't he his father's son too. Sure he has a father. He has seen the grave in Texas.

Watson's head jerks back, his eyes snap open. What the hell, he says, looking around. Do you take me for a fool?

He reaches for his pistol, but Watson doesn't go anywhere, the head soon enough nodding, the great gray eyes that Pearl so admires shutting, the breath coming deep and steady. Out there ahead ride Pearl and Jim July. He keeps his eye on them two. Anything can happen, his mama's right.

Sometimes he goes to the caves by himself, climbs the rocks to the highest one and walks far back into it, until the walls are scarce farther apart than the width of his shoulders and he must crawl to go farther. Summers it is a cool place, and quiet. He hides from Pearl, who, afraid to lose sight of the light, won't come past the first turn. His mother comes here with the fiddler. He watches her climb the rocks, the fiddler coming along behind, the fiddle strapped to his back in a shiny black case. Then he hears the music, the quick reels and jigs, and the laughing, hers and the man's, and then the slow airs that bring tears to his eyes. If he might make such sounds, if he could play a fiddle like that, why, everything would be all right. Flat on his back, he stares up through the flickering leaves to the sky, the fiddle tunes echoing from the cave like they was sung by the rocks. He never wants to leave, but then his mother calls him. Listen, she says, I want you to know about your father. He was a good man that the times drove to desperation.

My daddy, Pearl says, was a bad man. He is in prison far in the North and they won't ever let him out. He is a Younger from Missouri. Mama loved him best of all. She told me so.

Pearl, her long gown like a thick curtain blowing across the flanks of the Indian pony, rides at first by his side, and then, when the moon is above the treeline, she joins Jim July. She is a sweet woman, says Watson. Feisty. Reminds me of her mama. In the moonlight Watson's face looks to be made of glass, his breath just a trick. In the mirror the room dances and his own face looks back at him as if it sees more than he can ever hope to. My name, he writes, is Edwin Reed. My mother is Belle Starr. My father Jim Reed is buried in McKinney, Texas. We are Missourians. Before that we are Virginians. But those places are no more. We belong here in the Territory. There is no place else for us. We will be buried in this dirt, all of us together in a single plot on our own land.

They come to a rise, a plateau, the trees sparser, patches of ground broad and flat. The sky at last, he sees, lightens in the east. It's very cold now, even though the wind isn't strong. The river will be edged with ice, a gray-white border as fragile-looking as Pearl's lace. She hands him the fiddle, his mama does, and says, It is yours now, but when the man has put the bow in his hand and showed him how to touch the strings with it, it is as though he holds something else, a stick, a twig. When I play the fiddle, the man says, I watch the dancers and I feel like I am inside their skin. I tell you, it is a fine feeling.

We will put it here, she says, beneath the bed, and, its black case lost or broke long ago, the fiddle goes in the traveling bag with Pearl's summer smocks and skirts. When he takes it out again, not to play but to hold, to look at and to remember the songs made by the fiddler, it smells like crinoline and calico and gingham, like the women who have danced to it, cheeks flushed, bright eyes flashing, his mother the best of all. Someday, she says, you may want to learn how to play this fiddle. It will be here for you when that time comes.

He polishes it with the soft brim of a sunbonnet, often, then for months forgets about it, one day remembers, finds it where it has always been, takes it out and looks into the grain of the wood beneath the hard and shining varnish, the dark spirals in the maple back, the even lines of the spruce top breaking sharp at the curves that make the sides. Then one day it is gone, the traveling bag with it, nothing at all left beneath the bed. What he figures is that Pearl has taken it. What she wants it for, he can't guess. She is at Grandma Reed's having her baby.

I hope never to see her again, his mother says. She doesn't mean it, he knows, will welcome Pearl back, find her a husband and suckle the baby herself if need be. Who is the son of a bitch, she asks. Tell me who got you this way, but Pearl won't say. It is between me and my maker, she says.

He begins to think the sun will never come up, just stay beneath the edge of the trees and give off a hazy, spiteful light. the ravines deepen into gorges, gulleys into ravines. The wind starts blowing. Awake, Watson leans forward like he is sniffing a scent. Day's breaking, he says. We must be close now.

Close to what. Eddy smells the river, feels his mother's cheek touch his, Pearl tug at him, pull him into the warm water of the Canadian. What is it that he has had, what can he hope to have again. Lord, it is the feel of skin that this territory makes you learn. I am living in myself, but in her too, and she in me.

Close to Fort Smith, yes, soon the chimneys will appear, the clapboard houses beyond the bluffs of the gentle curving river.

Out of the Territory and into the State of Arkansas. A hearing for Watson. Pearl and Jim July wait at the bend, their horses nibbling at the high frost-edged needlegrass.

Morning, says Pearl.

Almost, says Watson.

The sun begins to slip above the branches of the trees. Higher, it is a deep red that makes Pearl's horse golden. Jim July's hair hangs to his shoulders in shining strands, and when Watson grins those white teeth look like they have caught fire.

Come on, Jim July says. Let's get this over and done with.

Watson will be let go though guilty, July chased after and shot down though innocent. Pearl will sell herself again and again to the men of Fort Smith, and his mama's tomb will be robbed of Cole Younger's pistol. Still it is a sweet moment back there on the trail at the border of the Territory, riding east into a winter sun so bright and warm. At that moment—and, taking up again her quill pen, he writes this down—I knew what it was to live. I shivered, knowing of all the ghosts afloat in my blood, liable to jam in that little stream at any time. Alive, I heard the dead earth whisper and my ghost heart sang its love into the risen wind, clear across to Arkansas. That river we crossed, there wasn't no bottom to it.

THE DEATH OF BELLE STARR

A Dream of Birds

That July feller. Hear tell he's a horse thief.

Watson talks loud, as if addressing a gathering, pronouncing each word with care, smiling broad enough to show the handiwork of his mouth. The teeth, Belle notices, are white all right, but the gums are gray and dull, like old felt, and his tongue slithers in his mouth like some plump rodent, pink and sleek, in a hole.

And what do you hear tell, she asks, about me, Mr. Watson.

Nothing. Nothing but good. But this July feller—

What you hear ain't necessarily what you want to believe.

Want to believe! Why, what matter is that, Mrs. Starr?

Just this. That log there. It is old and rotting. It is hollow. Kick it and it will split in two, it will fall open. But it is true.

It is neither here nor there.

Yes. It is both.

Fact is, Ma'am, you are avoiding my question.

We are all horse thieves, Mr. Watson. At heart.

Mebbe so. Mebbe not. But he done it with his two hands, heart be damned.

Tell me something I don't already know.

There is not a jealous bone in Jim July's body. The way he looks at it, he has been favored, he has been blessed, he has been allowed love. And what has he done to deserve it? Nothing. It happens to him before he knows it is happening, and when it happens it is as though he has been waiting just for this all his life. Well, well, he thinks, so this is who I am.

To Pearl he says, Keep your hands off of me. I belong to your mama.

I am a grown woman, she says, eighteen year old.

He knows that. Knows she's already a mama herself, her baby safe up in Missouri with Grandma Reed. But he knows it ain't his baby, and none of them are going to be his if he can help it.

Pearl, he says, I am practically your daddy.

How old are you, Jim July.

How old I am don't matter. I am your mama's man.

You ain't married to her. She won't have your name.

I have taken her name for my own. Jim July Starr. I belong to her.

It ain't the same, honey.

What if I tell her what you have been up to, Pearl. Then you will see what your mama has to say on this subject.

May be. Only you won't do that, will you.

I am not a betrayer by nature, but do not tempt me, sweetheart.

I like to tempt. It is *my* nature to tempt. I get it from *her*, I guess.

I belong to Belle Starr. It's not jealousy he feels when he sees Belle standing close to Watson, talking low, sauntering through the shade of the cottonwoods that line the creekbank. It's a chill, a shiver that seems to slow the flow of his blood and at the same time ram wind straight to his heart. She will not betray him, no. But he will be betrayed all the same. He steps back into the shadows of the trees, lights out for the path to the caves. He will feel her presence there, the warmth of her skin in the dark rocks, the motion of her soul in the cool air.

Pearl watches Watson from the trees. She sees him sitting on his porch, whittling, his wife Mandy stiff as a stump by his side. Occasionally he spits, usually straight ahead but sometimes towards Mandy, the dark stream, it looks like, just missing her boots. He's a tall man, almost as tall, she reckons, as old Tom Starr, and with the same lowdown meanness in the eyes. It is a kind of man she aims to understand. They are haters, she knows, driven and desperate. Still they draw her to them. Usually it is a little gesture that does it, a tilt of the head as though it is too heavy a load to carry, a way of dragging their heels over the dirt without stirring it up, or a squinty grin, a mouth drawn up tight as a pouch above a long and bristled chin. With him maybe it is them little teeth, spaced far apart and white as dogwood petals, some of them chipped, like they was really too delicate to eat with. It's always her mama they take a interest in. What a shame. What a pity.

On the first day Mandy sits in the buggy and surveys the surrounding trees, small they are but lush enough, not so tall as the trees in Arkansas but not enough difference really to matter. She is content. Edgar is going to be a farmer. Miracles never cease! And if they don't make it here, why, the territory to the west will soon be opened for settlement, and it is said that out there is the best land of all, no plough ever yet dug into it. He amazes her, her Watson. What isn't he capable of doing. Nothing. And so secret. Always he seems to be holding something back. What does she know about him—why, the contours of his body, the way the muscle rises hard and curving on the bone, the shape of his shoulders, ridged delicate like distant plateaus that you can reach out and touch. Just this and no more, and it has always been enough.

Well now, she says when he comes out. Did you find out what you wanted to know.

He looks down, he looks angry, he bites off a chaw. Yep, he says. And then the woman comes out, the door slamming shut behind her with a sharp whack like rifle fire in the woods. She steps towards their buggy, the hem of her gown trailing in the dust, her arms swinging brisk as a rag doll's. It is a swagger, Mandy thinks. Here is a woman who walks with a swagger. That means she will not be easy to know. It is too bad. Neighbors should be friends, and, anyway, who else is there? This is no country for women, not yet. It hasn't had the time. It ain't as civilized as Arkansas.

Eddy sees his mama drifting away from him, from all of them. These are the times she has gone away. He remembers waking in a dark room, hearing the hoofbeats grow softer, the next morning one of the Starr women, old Tom's Kate most likely, sitting in the rocker by the stove if it is winter, out under the simmon tree if summer, her face at all times the same, the color and texture of an old boot, riverbottom brown and much creased, a loose fit for the skull that has to wear it. Later there is no one at all. He is old enough to look out for himself. Belle has told him so and he believes it. He sits alone in the cabin, on her side of it, her room quiet and cool. When she marries Sam Starr, she says You're still Mama's favorite man. Ten years old at the time, he doesn't believe her. He watches her face when she says the vows. There is a smile he's not accustomed to seeing, a brightness in her eyes. Tom Starr stands beside his son, a lump in his cheek the size of a plum, his gaze fixed on the line of tattered clouds passing over the treetops. He's a head taller than the next tallest there, and he wears a high-topped beaver hat to boot, so that to Eddy he looks like God himself—save the tobacco-swollen cheek—an earthbound god anyway. I seen taller men in Missouri, Pearl says. I seen men tall as the trees in Missouri. Hush, says Eddy. Ain't I been to Missouri, too? Pearl makes circles in the dust with the toe of her boot. When the fiddle starts up, she lifts the hem of her skirt to her knees and pulls him onto the platform. Swing me hard, she says. Swing me hard, Eddy. I love that music. His mama's the one the men watch. Even if it wasn't her wedding, she's the one they'd be watching, concentrating on. The fiddler keeps his eyes on her while he plays, and you think she's who he's playing to, she's who the song is made for.

Watson dreams of birds. They squat on every stone, peck at the dirt, their wings hunched like shoulders. Among them, stretched out on her back like a corpse, his mama sleeps. But she says, Edgar, you have work to do, I believe, don't you, and the birds start flapping their wings, making a terrible sound. What in God's name is he to do. His mama's quiet now, or else drowned out by the noise of the birds, loud as a locomotive in the next room. He turns and there's a great dark hole in the ground waiting for him to walk into it. The birds fly over it, screaming, their wings wide as clouds. Another step and he's a goner. Now his mama's on her feet. She's *in* that damn hole! Git, she says. Didn't I tell you, Son, git.

Oh, but listen. She ain't in this room. That sound ain't nothing but the wind a-howling. This is Mandy asleep by your side, not Belle Starr. What is it you have got to do that your own mama, dead these ten years, won't let you be.

The Heart, the Blood

Mandy wonders. Sometimes Edgar is just not there. He's sitting at the table spooning beans into his mouth, careful and prim, but he's just not there. Talk to him or talk to the wall, it's all the same. Still, she can't help but think she's better off when he's this way. When he *is* here, when his soul ain't somewhere else, why, you never know what to expect. Meanness, like as not, some kind of meanness. No use to think about that. He has pleasing hands, don't he. He has some sweetness to him. That hardness, them eyes black as pitch, the slant of his thighs, the waist trim (though you dassn't say this to him) almost like a lady's, and other qualities she won't mention but pleasing all the same. Edgar Watson. Only it's Bob she's to call him now. She mustn't forget. It surely would not do to make him angry with her, and goodness knows it makes no difference to her what he calls himself. She knows who he is.

Up in Catoosa the men give Eddy a hard time.

Well, they say, if it ain't the son of the Outlaw Queen.

Make room, boys. Here's Eddy, Belle's boy, come to hold us up.

Eddy, where's your mama. Riding with the James Boys?

He pays them no mind. He takes his whisky straight. There's a darkness in him, and when he feels it there's nothing but to get out, get away from her, from Pearl too. The trouble is, he sees too much, everything edged with evil. Malice afoot. Greed out of hand, greed without no object, greed for its own sake. It is what we are made of, what we smell of.

Boys, he says. I come here to Catoosa out of a dire need, and that need is—to celebrate!

Is she getting married again.

Is Jim July run off with Pearl.

Has Judge Parker strung your mama up.

Have you stole her mare again.

Has old Tom Starr gone to hell to meet his maker.

Is Cole Younger escaped from jail and come after his Belle.

No, boys. I celebrate nothing in particular.

Hurrah for nothin in particler! More of the same!

More of the same, Amen!

On horseback Belle comes to the clearing. This forest, she thinks, has been my life, dark and true, with few trails coming into it and fewer coming out. I sit astride when I ride through these trees, the horse's heat pushing against the leather of the saddle like fingers. It seems like I have been here all my life. Nothing is changed, changing, the sun lighting the tips of them last brown leaves like always, the slant of the sun through the plum-color clouds the same. I have been somewhere, I have someplace to go to, it hasn't been a meaningless errand.

She stops, listens. There is a roaring in the air, as if, not far away, water plunges over a cliff, splashes onto rock.

Watson clears his throat, kicks at a rock, stuffs his hands deep in his pockets. The sky, Belle observes, is in motion, clouds crossing in a hurry, and the tops of the trees begin to whip back and forth. It has been a mild winter, but it is not over yet. February awaits us. March is getting ready.

I'll tell you, Watson says. I know more'n you think.

Speak then.

Words fail me. Words won't say all I know.

It is a common failing.

Sometimes I think I know more'n anybody knows.

That is also a common failing.

You turn my words against me. You hear what you want to.

But what, after all, *does* he know. Precious little, she'd say. He knows of people's doings—so he says, but what count is that? There is another truth, another knowing. It is of the heart, it is of the blood. It is how we are and why. It makes us more than flesh. She, for example, is not even here, though her body fill the space by his side, though the soles of her boots make arrows in the light sleet that coats the path. This is her ghost, flesh though it be, and her other self, the one of the heart and the blood, steps into a clearing in the woods, alone, and does not ever want to leave that sudden warmth, that leaf-soft light. She will build a cabin there and live in it. Already she is living in it.

You will allow, won't you, Mama, as to the possibility, howsomever slight, just the nariest possibility that there's evil abroad in the world?
Surely. It is in the eye of the beholder.
It is in everybody's eye.
There is a mote in your eye, Eddy.
You like that Watson, don't you. You want to make him love you.
Certain things about him I admire.
Certain things!
That lope. That little grin.
I give up on you, Mama. I wash my hands of you. I rue the day I stepped into this world.
Wasn't much of a step, Eddy. I'm not talking to you no more.
More like a slide, somewhat like a surge, out, then back in, like you was beating a retreat. Now your sister Pearl, she was the quick stepper. She came into this world on the run, as I remember. You hesitated, Son.

Edgar has taken to spending a good deal of time with his shotgun. An inordinate amount of time, Mandy would say. Shining it. Peering through its barrels like he was looking through opera glasses. Rubbing, rubbing. Seeing himself in that gunmetal, like as not. She could see herself too if she cared to look, which she most definitely does not. Does it matter to them poor squirrels, she would say to him, that they was killed with a shotgun that the barrels shine like a mirror? Do them rattlers you say you keep running into appreciate so pretty a gun aiming at them? Edgar,

Edgar. What has come of us. You wasn't always so mean. And I, I know, I wasn't always so low, my spirits were most high in former times. When we had that little house in Blue Mountain, Arkansas, the past left behind us: a new life, Mandy, you said to me. We are starting afresh. I believed in you. I believed in us. The wind blowing through those Arkansas trees was sweet to me, honey. There was nothing else, you made me forget everything: my dead brother, my lost son—that was all behind us, and it was just you and me. I wish I knew what drew you to this God-forsaken spot. I wish to God you never heard a word said about this Territory.

The Clearing

Pearl is biding her time. Let Eddy do what he pleases, ride off to Catoosa on their mama's favorite horse, Belle's darling Venus, see if she cares when he comes back and gets a whipping for it. I am old enough to have my own life, he says. She knows what Belle will say about that: You are old enough to have it on your own horse! The trouble with Eddy is he's got no common sense. Sam Starr never could do nothing with him, and his own daddy Jim Reed was shot dead before Eddy could have the advantage of his advice. Not that Jim Reed's advice would've amounted to much! She doubts it. As for her, she'll never take no one's advice. It never applies, that is her experience. What happened before don't happen again the same way, and so how can anyone tell you anything that will make a difference, one way or the other? Something's wrong, Eddy says. It's a bad deal the world makes us. She knows better. It's no deal at all. Nothing's for sale. You got to steal. What you want you got to steal.

I'm talking about the soul, says Eddy.

Does he think she is talking about horses?

They drink and Eddy drinks, watching them drink. Oh, it's a fine thing, ain't it, to be here in Catoosa amongst these gentlemen. Decent fellows! They know him and they accept him and this is what he is, this dark figure in the mirror, a mustache thickening above his womanish lips. There might be, he reckons, a trace of his daddy in that image, dead Jim Reed that rode with Quantrill and Jesse James. But mainly it is Belle Starr looking back at him from that glass. He's his mama's boy, no getting around it.

What is the good word from Younger's Bend, Eddy?

Mama's gone off to Fort Smith. She's taking July in.

Taking him in, is she. Well.

They got nothing on him, she says.

I reckon.

She'll come back and wait.

The usual procedure.

Yep. It's happened before.

Ha! I reckon. More of the same.

I was in prison once, Jim. It wasn't so bad. I learned how to cane a chair. In a year I was back in the Territory with Sam Starr.

I remember.

Then before I knew it, Sam was dead, killed by a coward, shot at a dance.

I was there, Belle.

There's some of us wasn't cut out for this world.

I am one of them.

There's nothing but to love every minute of it.

I always thought so myself.

I remember everything ever happened to me. What I forgot, I remembered in that prison, and I haven't forgot any of it since then.

I remember the time you and Sam saw me in the wagon. I had

a splinter in my finger. You looked over the sideboard and I thought it was a angel come to take me away. Then I saw Sam and knew you. I was a child but just like I am today. Jim then, Jim now.

I remember Cole Younger. He had such long fingers.

I remember some of what never happened to me. I remember what happened to my grandfather because I have heard the stories. Riding a gray pony, he left the eastern lands of the Creek. The sky was bright that day, and the clouds moved rapidly across it, fleecy and pale. It was a long journey that no one wanted to make. Along the way was much weeping. Many died and were buried in strange country.

In my family there was also a journey. Our way was from Missouri to Texas, across the Territory. Jim Lane and his redlegs chased us out. The War raged in Missouri, but in the Territory I noticed the hawks afloat in the sky and heard the jays calling across the treetops. In Texas it was dry and dusty. I remembered the Territory I had passed through and I swore to return. Soon afterwards I met Cole Younger. I was not yet eighteen. He treated me like I was a lady. Honey, he said, you remind me of my little sister. Now he is in prison, and I am still here in the Territory.

There is no place else for the Creek. The old men talk of a return some day, but there will be no going back to that place. Here is where we will remain.

Here is where I'll stay.

There's no other home for me.

I have no regrets.

Me neither.

But they won't let us stay.

No. Nothing never stays put.

We'll have another Missouri to cross.

Another homeland to leave.

Another trail, another river.
Always the sky, the trees.
Something to endure.
Maybe we'll end up in Texas.

Mandy has a bad dream. Edgar rides towards her in a cloud of dust. She can see only his head, how he is grinning at her like he means to bring her good news. But he's ever so far away, and the dust makes it harder and harder to see him. Yes, she says to Belle Starr, he did kill my brother, but that was only a terrible accident. At heart he is a decent man. He means good. There's kindness in his soul. Belle seems not to hear. She is aiming her pistol at Edgar. Mandy has never seen the likes of that pistol. Why, it looks more like a fiddle! You couldn't hurt nobody with that. But the fiddle is fired, and Edgar, just before he falls, looks at her, his Mandy, like it was *her* fault. Edgar, she cries, running towards the spot where he lies stretched out on the grass stiff and straight as a fence post, Edgar honey, I never blamed you for what happened. Not for one minute. Then when she gets to him, he's tiny, he's a baby someone's left behind, he's got the soft sweet face of a baby, but she knows it's him because it's his teeth in the little mouth. More happens, she can't remember what all else, but she keeps remembering him like that, a babe in the grass that someone has left behind, not a bit like himself but for them perfect little teeth, looking for all the world like they was carved by human hand.

When Pearl comes to the clearing, her first thought is that nothing at all has happened. It is a joke that Eddy has dreamed up. Her mama shot! Why, that woman's skin is hard as iron, you can't kill her with a bullet, you will have to melt her down and there ain't a fire with sufficient heat for the task. But here's Frog Hoyt pulling on her arm, and there's tears coursing down his cheeks, mighty fine pretending if Eddy's only put him up to this stunt. Then she sees—her mama seated on the ground, her back against the trunk of a scrawny blackjack. There is the mare Venus, tied to a branch, rubbing the side of its head against the upper part of the trunk.

I came running soon's I heard that shot, Frog Hoyt says. It was loud as thunder and I says to myself, Milo, I says, something bad has happened. And I lit out. When I come to her, she was face down in the mud, and Venus was whining like a scared hound, standing in just that same place. Lord, I says, it is Belle Starr shot deader than a doornail. And I drug her to this tree and sat her up here where you see her, and then I run straight for you, Pearl honey. Lord, that's all I know. I don't even know if she's dead or alive.

Pearl kneels, looks her mama in the eye. Nothing. Mud drying in her hair. Touch her and she's cold. Turn her over and there's a dozen dark spots on the back of her riding jacket. They look like little flowers.

Mama, you've got yourself a mess of trouble now.

What I mean for you to know, Watson says, is this: you and me, we was meant for each other. I know it. Oh, I know. You been told that before. You heard that plenty of times. I know all about you. I would not be here right now, walking in this damn wind, if I did not know.

I'm claimed, Mr. Watson. And so are you.

Mebbe. But I got rights, what I know.

Are we talking about love, or what.

We are talking about you and me.

Then we are talking about nothing.

The hell you say. I know you better than you think.

What I think don't matter. Nor what you think you know.

Across the river she sees the light moving in the trees, swift, like it was chasing shadows or being chased. A strange dance, she thinks, and I am part of it. Beyond the trees is my clearing. I hear a fiddle playing, the prettiest sound I ever heard. It is not a human sound, no human being can make such music as that, it is the sound the wind is always trying to make, it is how the cottonwoods want their leaves to sing: *Love, I'm listening. I hear.*

And Watson says: I am older than the trees.

II
FINDING JESSE JAMES

QUANTRILL

Almost asleep, he remembers how from the beginning it is a gray morning, a morning for sleep. Back of the barn the pond glimmers, its smooth surface undisturbed by the fine mist, and the barn, with small louvered windows and a high sloped roof jutting outwards a good fifteen feet all around, looks big and safe as a fort. Stepping through the wide doorway, into the warm smell of hay and horses, he hears talking, but it is distant. His father's voice—impossible. This is Kentucky. He's going up Salt River to Louisville, and his father's in Ohio, dead these eight, these ten years. Now he's the teacher, not his father, and so the voices are *his* scholars. Men, he tells them, we can't keep this up forever. They aren't listening. They sleep. Stretched out in the piles of hay in the fodderloft, they look like reflections of himself. Anderson's dead. And Todd. Many more have been lost. Brother MacLindley, Clarke, beloved sister Cornelia Lisette. Thomas Henry Quantrill, father, sadly missed. Himself next.

They've taken his boots, stolen them when he can do nothing to prevent it, lying in the mud with a ball in his back. Thieves of the worst kind. Is this, he wonders, the kind of treatment an officer can expect in Kentucky.

Look, my son, to a higher court.

He lies down, wants to rest, wants to be let alone. Only there's little room. He goes into the shed and there's his father, swinging the strop. *Uhn, uhn*. It was hard work, yes, all of it hard work, and the sooner he understood that simple fact the better.

Dark, the shed smells like leather. Around him hang the straps, the heavy buckles. Confess? What shall he confess. He has been a bad boy, Father. He has sinned most shamelessly. There is lust aplenty and more pride than he needs. *I have come to save your soul.*

Hard work.

The moment can't be brought back. That's the trouble. Blink and there's another upon us. Why, he wonders, does that have to be so.

The man has no answers. He smells of strong soap. You are in Louisville, Captain Quantrill, in a hospital. So the man says. Others too. But he knows better. The buckles jingle ever so slightly at the end of the long thick strips of leather. The sound annoys him, keeps him from sleep. He would like to rest, lie here among his men and get some sleep. The hay is soft, the rain silent. But that infernal jingling! That damnable priest! What next. His mother? Lord help us.

No. Not his mother. Nor is it Kate. This is another woman. He can just make her out on the other side of the window, just beyond the passing reflection of his own ghostly face, a still figure in a dark room, her face pale, eyes opened wide as though she is looking on something she never expected to see, some shocking sight. Is she afraid of him? Why, he's just a man like any other, no more, no less. He'd stop if he might, hitch up this horse and pay her a little visit. She'd see. He would behave like a gentleman.

The truth is, he begins to lose interest in this struggle. He would like to rest, take a holiday. Let Bill Anderson and George Todd do all the bloody work. But they are dead—so he's been told. Well, he's had enough of their company. Bring him Kate. Wasn't that a fine summer they had though, he and Kate hiding away deep down in Howard County while all around them the men of the Colorado Calvary, their blue uniforms ragged and dusty, lurk and search and never see a thing.

Here they come!

And he must run, no time to fool with a damn skittery horse made wild by the sound of gunshots. Just get out of here, get to the brush. The ground is sodden, slippery. Ahead of him horses leap the fence. He follows them. The rain comes heavier now. What a day to be chased out of a warm dry hayloft! He remembers the dark slippery roots, hard and sprawled across the pathway like big fingers, and the men up ahead beckoning from their rearing horses. Good men! They love him, they will risk their own lives to save him, their Captain, their Charley Quantrill. Give up this? Never. Where is Kate. Bring him Kate. He wants to tell her he loves her.

Hiding in the barn, she presses against him, her skin like nothing else that has ever touched him, warmer and softer and pleasanter. The hard smell of hay mixes with the soft scent of flowers in her hair. In the intervals that the birds stop twittering —brief moments, surely, but growing longer in his remembering them—he can hear the smooth breathing of the horses in the stalls below. We're safe, ain't we, she asks, and he says yes, safe as we'll ever need to be.

It's almost over, don't you think.

Yes, I surely hope so.

And what will it be like—afterwards? Like before?

How was that.

His father stands in front of the room in the schoolhouse, his willowstick pointer aimed at a word on the blackboard, his black coat lightened at the cuffs by chalkdust. *William must know the answer. Ask him.* Outside, the leaves flicker like eyelids and behind them a lusterless sky darkens. This the early autumn before the long illness. He does not mean to be impudent. Sir! He *was* paying attention. But he can't remember the word, the word his father points to. Not for the life of him can he remember.

It's not necessary to remember everything. Nor should it matter that he has lost all strength, all desire to move. He is one with the body of Christ Our Savior, and *that* body surely races hell-bent, lickety-split from tree to tree, no ball fast enough to fetch it back to the damp earth, no root slippery enough to trip it up.

Grace isn't the word his father points to on the blackboard. Perhaps the word is for the spelling list: *conceive*, as in Conceive of this, that a man brought forth in... notice the *e* before the *i*. This illustrates a fundamental rule, a basic principle. His father does not smile, his face perfectly smooth, with neither line nor hollow, as though pure flesh, no bones beneath. Perhaps it is a number that he points to, the answer to a calculation. *The Principles of Higher Mathematics*. The book is dusty, leaves yellowing at the edges. Thank God Mama loves him, her first born, her William, her boy Bill. Thinking of her, he leaps onto the back of the horse, slips, can't get up, and then they're taking his boots and he can't do a thing to stop them.

Like anyone else in these days, he wants to make his fortune. His father dead, he stands before those scholars in that cold schoolhouse out in Indiana and says to himself, even while pressing the soft chalk onto the blackboard, I am not that man. That man is dead and does not live on through me, his son. God the Father forgives, yes, but it's this one that won't let up, this man dead but in my blood, in my throat, I hear his voice when I speak. *Turn, please, to page seventy-six.* It is cold. They would huddle around the squat black stove, let their small hands hover close to the hot cast iron, but no, he'll not permit it. Keep the mind active and the body will take care of itself. That is his father speaking, not him, not son William, though the words issue from his mouth, though his own hands are so cold he can scarce grip chalk or pointer and his own mind feels barren, the wind whistling through his skull and blowing clean away the layers of philosophy and fact he has so prudently laid up these many months.

People are talking about Kansas. In the West a man could make good, start afresh, stake his claim. That's what they're saying around the fires, eyes glowing.

His claim to what. Tell him, please. *Grace*. The man sits by his side, does he never leave, does he never eat sleep slop, this small red-faced man, this solemn wit, this father. *The miracle is that Christ the Son of God of Man is mortal immortal*. Mortal like you and me. Mortality's the mystery, ain't it. This flesh that's our fortune and downfall. Why don't it last. Principle of life be damned. Give him life unprincipled, unschooled. Learning's a lie. The old man, Mr. Thomas Henry Quantrill, knew that, taught it every day of his life to all his scholars and children, a hard lesson it is, but one that stays with you, with sons and daughters everywhere.

Still there is Kansas out there. Land as fresh and tantalizing as a woman's skin, Kate's skin, you want to touch it, you want to lie atop it and press your cheek into its furrows. Sweet dark soil! She lies beside him and whispers, Charley, I don't ever want to leave here, all around them the bluecoats swarming. He is a patriot, a lover of this land, governments be damned, he loves all of it, Kansas and Missouri alike, the Indian Territory with its blood-colored dirt and squat trees and stunted hills. He looks forward to returning his flesh to this land, cares not a whit whether it's Missouri or Kentucky that claims him. He's ready to give himself up, but can't move a muscle, nothing left of him but this tongue to wag, and nothing to say. Everything to say. But where to find the words. Lord help him. Is he looking into a mirror or through a window. The face is his own, but not the expression, as though somebody's climbed into his skin and found it to fit. Smiles back at him who is left behind.

But no, it's only his father. Now Father wipes the yellowish pane with his broad palm and leans closer, the sky behind him cloudless and bright. He wants to be certain I've not left the shed before my time is up. When he sees, then he'll return to the house, pull his chair close to the fire and reach for the flames. Is he still there, Mother asks. He's still there all right. He can't move, not an inch. It grows darker and the wind stabs its way through the chinks, sharp with the chill of November. He thinks: I could learn to like it here. I could stay here all the time if I had to. Far away a horse whinnies. *Here they come!*

He runs for his life. He won't be imprisoned in a dingy schoolhouse for his allotted time on this earth, not with all that territory out there waiting to be claimed. A man can make a fortune for himself. In Kansas. *Wait up, men!*

Lincoln's dead, but the way it looks to him it makes no difference. They must make their way to Virginia, to Lee, and be on hand when the surrender—and the pardon—occurs. In the West there will be no mercy. They'll all be in bad trouble in Missouri, in Kansas. Todd was shot dead, and Anderson too. Do you think there'll be mercy for Captain Quantrill's boys!

Frank James will come with him. And Parmer. Payne Jones, the Pence boys, Jim Younger, Dick Burns. Thirty others at least. Who needs more. Now let's go up Salt River. That's good country, plenty of good sympathetic people to help along the way.

He wants his mother to know that he has arrived in God's Country. The fields stretch endlessly westward, gleam in the bright sunshine, the soil so rich and dark that the grasses grow wild and blow in the wind like ripples in a broad river. He has walked through those grasses and felt the clean new air filling his lungs, satisfying as food. *This is God's palm that I walk on now. I will send for you soon, Mother. My prospects are good.*

And so they go up Salt River and come to this place. Wakefield's. Knobby country but with plenty of good bottomland. Build your house high and farm in the lowland. This is old Kentucky, the faces looking out at you through the farmhouse windows worn thin and yellow, the eyes like pieces of iron, like his mother's eyes, and when he rides he sees her in those cabins, him there too, Father in his deathbed, and he wants to say Boys, let's give up, let's turn ourselves in, ask for mercy. It's the only hope left for us. Let's surrender. Let's turn back towards our homes.

Up Salt River the trees droop heavy with bright green leaves of early spring. His horse is his home, warm and slick and rippling between his legs, the thud of the hooves against the hard ground like fat raindrops splashing onto that sod house roof back in Kansas, the woman looking out the window watching for him, waiting. She has the food he's hungry for. He smells it even now, the trees passing beside him as if in review, straight and tall now; he smells the bacon frying in her pan, the bread in her oven, earth her hearth, floor, roof, giving off a scent as of woman herself, all women. My God, how he has loved her. Even now, riding through these stately trees, he's overcome with desire, it hits him as sudden as that ball in his back, renders him just as useless in another place and time, that room with its flickering lamp, its high arching windows, outside the unmoving darkness, the black Kansas sky. Blessed Redeemer! Mother, pray for me. I want to be good, I want to be a good man, worth loving, worthy to give love.

> *My horse is at the door*
> *And the enemy I soon may see*
> *But before I go Miss Katy*
> *Here's a double health to thee—*

It's Terrill's Raiders who are about. A scoundrel, says Wakefield, that fights only when adequately whisky'd. A mere youth of nineteen, a coward. Watch for him back of the trees, listen for the soft hoofbeats of his swift horses. But surely in this barn, the rain steady now, heavier, and beating on the tin roof as though it will never quit, the men of Captain Quantrill can sleep safe, take their ease in the hayloft and dream of their women.

And what will it be like afterwards—like before?

What was it like then. Tell him that, please. No peace ever, save at moments like these, when present and future stop chasing you and you're set afloat in memory without a paddle. Up Salt River you can make your way through these bright hills eastward and say at last, I give up. I surrender. I ask for mercy. If only that moment will stay put.

So this is what it amounts to. Trouble. A doctor and a priest, both saying, You are mortal, mortally wounded. Make your peace. He has some feeling in his hands, would like once again to touch, caress, but damn it, look now, they've even shot off one of his fingers. He lies still, won't get up from this bed of mud, couldn't even if he wanted to. They'll have to carry him back to Wakefield's or, if he don't live long enough, bury him here in this Kentucky mud. Yes, Lord, yes, take his boots. He won't be needing them any longer. Everybody wants a memento, a souvenir. These boots, tell them, belonged to William Clarke Quantrill. He was wearing them when he received his mortal wound. Yes, take them, yank them off, be quick about it, can't use them anymore, can't feel a thing down there, neither cold nor pain.

They take his boots, his pistols. They carry him back to the farmhouse. This much he knows. Terrill's men move like cats from room to room. If he could move, he could escape.

Say, look at this jug. Ahma take this back home to Mama!

They're young. This one looks like a pupil of his, a big boy with a mouthful of gray teeth, won't learn a thing, says it won't help him what he aims to do. Too big to whip, but you can catch him out by the sugar orchard and lay into him before he knows what's hitting him.

Looting's their right, but Wakefield knows how to handle them, pays them off with a little cash, a little whisky. They don't get off with much.

This is Quantrill, ain't it.

Don't believe it is, no. Calls himself Captain Clarke. A pleasant fellow.

Pleasant! Why, he's a murderer, a thief, a rebel.

These are troubled times. Who's to say why a fellow turns out the way he does.

See that he stays where he is, hear?

He's in no condition to get up and go someplace, sir.

He's Quantrill. I know he's Quantrill from out Missouri.

William, his father calls him. *Bill*, his mother. *Charley*, he says, call me Charley, and it's just like you're a new man, you've got another life out there in the West, nobody knowing who you are so that you see that you can do anything and that is what you'll be, not what you were but what you are.

He's Quantrill. Don't trust him an inch.

Even if he wants to, he's not going anywhere.

Someone might come carry him off in the night, some of his men that got away.

So this is what it is to have no body. He can think—Lord, can he think—but let him try to wiggle a toe. He has fingers for touching, for gripping and squeezing, and can stroke the cold sheets he's been wrapped in, but let him try to touch the skin of his thigh, feel his chest's hard flesh. You might as well finger a table. Why, he's pure soul. He keeps his wits about him. In the dark he listens, he won't sleep—rest his legs? they're resting—he hears the hootowl. Is that Frank James. Buck, is that you? He hears breathing in the walls, a weeping in the windows. He wants Buck to get back his boots, for though his feet ain't cold and he plans no hike for freedom, he wants the boots back on his feet. Souvenirs, by God, but for himself. Of himself, for himself. And the pistols. The pistols'll bring a good price. Send the money to his mother, who once sent him a good pair of boots all the way out to Kansas, paying good money for them, he can tell, for the leather's fine, dark and supple, and the soles thick as planks. There's somebody in that family eating less so that she can send him these boots, and God arranges for the faces of sickly Franklin and frail Mary, their eyes dark as he imagines his own soul to be, to look down on him in reproach all one long night from the weedy roof above his head. The boots don't even fit. She'd thought he'd grown. He supposes she thinks he will keep on growing as fast away from her as by her side. The boots are two sizes too big. He gets a good price for them and means to send her the money.

And what, may I ask, did you use the money for?

Who's asking. By what right does he claim to know, this man coming to him with questions. Money? Yes, he's got money. Send it to Kate. Put a stone over his grave. Pray for him. These are not idle words. He wants his body back, that frame of muscle and blood he's learned to live with, that temple of the Lord sacked by Terrill's gang. *We will receive our reward in the flesh, just as we have suffered during this life in the flesh.* Think of that. He is thinking of it. It sounds too good to be true. Yet the man looks honest enough, sitting beside him in a Shaker chair, leaning forward slightly, his black garb clean and bright in this room of ever-shifting shadows, his red face nodding as though it were on a tightly coiled spring, his voice almost a whisper, saying Louisville, you've been brought to Louisville, mortally wounded.

The room has low ceilings. With its dirt floor and dank air it is more like a cellar than a parlor, but its windows let in sunlight, and through them he sees the long treeless plain and its wild and blowing grasses. A woman enters. Her dark skirt, shining and many tiered, sweeps across the floor around her as though preparing the surface for the touch of her feet. William, she says, will you come this way. She turns and he follows her through the door, not recognizing her but drawn to her and curious as to what she has in mind for him. He is surprised to see that she steps immediately into a forest. Why hasn't he noticed this forest before. The trees are tall, so thick with leaves that the light is dim and it is difficult to make one's way. Where are we going, he asks the woman. To meet your mother, she says. She walks by his side now, has taken hold of his hand and squeezes it gently. He would like to take her in his arms, or be taken in hers, forget about his mother, but she walks on. In her free hand, he now notices, she carries a pair of boots. His? He can't be sure.

He can't be sure of anything though. Where, for example, is he? In himself. He's no coward, but now he's frightened. He has the feeling that he's being carried somewhere — too fast, carelessly, as though he were a bag of potatoes. Afterwards, he tells Kate, it will be the same as before. We will be older, that's all, those of us who live through it. But now he's not so sure. Have faith, the man tells him. Ask for it, pray for it. Repent and you will be forgiven. He's heard that before. She's raised him a good Christian, clutched his hand and pulled him along with her to the Presbyterian Church, where he sits on the hard pew and stares at the yellow curls in front of him and hears more than he knows he's going to remember. I am the Resurrection and the Life, isn't that the way it goes, the voices droning, he'd as soon be outside, anywhere else but here in this room crowded up against mortal sinners, their heavy breathing worse than the sound of the wind coming through the chinks, as though the room itself wheezes, then moans. His father turns, writes the word on the blackboard, but all he can see is the man's back, the long dark coat like a curtain, worn but still not admitting light. How can it be any darker. Yet it darkens even as he listens to the sound of the chalk pressing against the surface of the slate, and when he turns he sees they are lifting his father from the bed to the casket. I intend, his father says, standing in the doorway of the shed, to pray for you. Don't you move now, until I tell you to. You stay right here.

He wants room to lie down, looks for his place among them, remembers movement, the sweat-slick horse leaping and galloping into the camp of the enemy, carrying him to the distant banks of swift-flowing rivers, bearing him steadily across the plains and into the caves, the wooded sanctuaries, towards the flickering lights of homes and villages faraway. He feels certain that that woman on the other side of the window is beckoning to him. She wants him to dismount, surrender. Have you any food for a hungry man, he wants to ask her. Later he will confess his love, beg mercy, promise faithfulness. Never has he felt such love! Men, he says, we must turn away from these sinful ways, live righteous, decent lives, return to our homes contrite, humble. Our pride has been our downfall.

They don't hear him. In that fodderloft they lie curled in their sleep, his wayward scholars, his fleeing soldiers, his longlost lovers. Bless him, Father, he's sleepy too. Love, a blanket for your cold Captain.

MRS. JESSE JAMES, MOURNING

1876–1881

He's a blue-eyed handsome man but he makes you worry. She watches him ride away, his linen duster flying and the dust sworling up behind him, and she thinks: this is to be my portion. A skillet. Little Jesse crying. Mary moaning. This plank floor and these thick windows, the bright fire, the distant trees. Zee, he says, I'm going. She knows, has known long ago. He comes in and paces. He wrings his hands. He stares, his blue eyes glazing over, then commencing to blink.

Stay here with me, she says.

Zee, I have got to go.

She knows, but regrets. Zerelda, his mother and her aunt and namesake, also regrets.

I see he's gone again, she says.

Yes, he's gone again.

Say where?

He never says.

No. He wouldn't.

She walks her mother-in-law to the door. The trees sway and clouds move across the sky as though in a great rush to get someplace else. The clouds look like great dark hands, big fists. She closes the door, fixes the latch, turns to her children, who are hungry, one crying, one tugging at her hand.

In Saratoga they ride out the long boulevard in a grand phaeton, past the mansions with the wonderful turrets and gracious porches, the driver sitting tall and rigid in front of them in a narrow-brimmed, flat-topped gray hat that she is certain will blow away in one of the warm gusts of wind but that remains firmly in place while she almost loses the scarf she's tied so carefully in a broad bow around her neck. Jesse wears the dark suit he's purchased in New York City. Quiet, he sits as rigid as the driver, his hands folded in his lap. You would think he sat in church, listened to a sermon. Wouldn't it be wonderful, she wants to say, to live in a home such as one of these. She sees herself moving from room to room, her silk gown rustling, Jesse in the parlor with his newspaper, his cigar, the children in the playroom two floors above, watched by a selfless nursemaid. She loves little Jesse, sweet Mary, but can she help it if she sometimes desires her husband, wants him all alone to herself, the way it used to be?

But of course it has never been as it should be. Not even now, in this fine carriage, is it as it should be. Look at him. What is he thinking, what is he feeling. Shouldn't she know, have some inkling. Why does he so seldom speak, take her into his confidence. There has been a time—but no, there hasn't been a time. Nothing has been provided. She must grasp, she must always be pulling at him, at life itself. He has no self. Don't his actions say as much? She believes everything she has ever heard about him. He is an outlaw, a thief. He has nothing of his own, not even a name.

At the baths the woman helps her down into the warm water. She thinks of Jesse, wonders what he thinks as he feels the water's warmth. No doubt nothing. Probably he thinks nothing at all, a secret even to himself. Is the water warm enough, the woman asks. It is very warm. Warm and calming. She lowers herself into it. I might drown, she thinks. I might let my head come with my body down into the water. Then I would be the mystery.

Aunt Zerelda waves the stump of her right arm as though it

were a stick. Zee, she says, men are all the same. Even my dear Dr. Samuel, why, he's no more with me sometimes than my dead father, just a memory of himself in the flesh. There's much we must resign ourselves to.

Little Jesse jumps at his grandmother when she comes, and Zee thinks he will knock her over surely, for he's a growing boy, heavy as sin, but Ma Zerelda clasps her good arm around him and lets him hang onto the other and together they stagger towards the high-back rocker. Tell me about the Pinkertons, he says. Tell me how they blew off your arm, Nanna. He has his father's tact, as well as his blue eyes and the same shuffling gait. Mary looks like her grandmother in the eyes, their sockets set back as if for better safety, and like her father in the mouth, the lips small in proportion to the chin and nose and customarily drawn tight. When I grow up, she says frequently, I'm going to marry a rich, rich man and live in a big house with tall trees all around it so that nobody can ever find us.

I won't think about him, she tells herself. He is dead to me and I will go on with my life. And she rides into town, the children left with their grandmother. She rides in the little cabriolet Jesse has brought her from St. Louis, rides with her head high, her hands tight around the thick reins. I'm permitting myself to be seen, she thinks. I want the gentlemen on Messanie Street to turn their heads when I pass. There goes a fine-looking woman, I want them to say, tipping their high-crowned hats.

He says it was the war that changed everything. That is what he used to say, his voice lowering so that it doesn't sound like a voice, the vowels firm as fruit fresh-picked. Before the war, he says, a man had a chance. There was rich farms. prosperous towns, and for them of a mind to seek fortune in other climes there was California and the promise of gold.

California. Hasn't his father gone to California. Left his mother behind with three young children. Gone and found nothing, sent nothing back. In fact never heard from again. And all this *before the war*.

Oh, he could be tiresome sometimes. Lord, yes. Before the war! Before the war indeed. Before the war as well as during it he was a boy, no man at all, hardly out of knee britches when the redlegs start their raiding and the federals their burning, scarce eighteen when Lee surrenders. But with two years of fighting with Quantrill's raiders, he points out, his blue eyes fierce and rapidly blinking, as if he suddenly sees the whole war again, everything all at once, the fire and the bloodshed, himself in the midst of it, pistols brandished and smoking. *I'm with child*, she tells him, and off he goes, not saying where, climbing onto the big horse, and she lies there alone in the bed and thinks maybe he is only a dream, everything that has happened to her since she has left the home of her parents in Kansas City a dream, this house on the hill, these children who survive and those poor dead twins, this child in her womb tinier surely than a finger, all a dream. She will wake up and there he will be, a man with Jesse's eyes—only they will not blink like his do. Unflinching, this man looks deep into her eyes and says, You are my life. Let me be yours. A lover to love, this one. An outlaw, perhaps, but alive, hidden in her heart.

Hotter, she tells the attendant. I want the water hotter. I want it steaming hot. And then he says, It's time, Zee. It's time we moved on. The baths make her feel as though she might live a life, after all, of perfect loveliness, in warmth, submerged but breathing fine. It's time, he says, and they are on the train again, headed south, the land through the windows passing as if it were in fact another kind of river, swift and dangerous to cross, whose dirt you might drown in.

She is with child, the fourth time in their marriage. When Jesse and Mary learn to walk, they move so like their father that she expects them to come to her any minute, say, Now it's time. We have got to move on. We don't know when we'll be back. They will not, she is certain, ever be able to stay put, doomed with a double dose of the blood that dooms their father, their uncle. Getting even takes a long time, at least a life. Young, lying wounded in her father's house, he tells her what has happened. They found me in the cornfield, he says. They was Jim Lane's men, come looking for Quantrill. Frank'd been riding with Quantrill, and I guess they found that out and so naturally came to us. But we wasn't saying a word. I lit out for the fields, nary a thought in my head about what fate I was leaving behind for my dear mother. I tore through them fields, run through the corn rows, and all the time I hear the horses tromping over the stalks and know it ain't no escaping. They get me down there all right, but I swear they'll pay. I'll be harder to find next time.

He could've been a preacher like his runaway daddy, yes, he could if he could only preach on the wrongs done to him and to his brother and to his beloved maimed mother. On that subject he might speak for hours and keep your attention.

She has heard him sing hymns, a pure and lovely tenor, when he comes to visit her, his cousin Zerelda Mims of Kansas City, and takes her to the Baptist Church, later to ride with her to the river, the Missouri, wider and bluer in those sweet summers before the war, with tufts of columbine and chicory spread across its banks like decoration put there for their pleasure alone. I am a family man, he tells her later, courting her while she nurses his war wound. I want to be a husband to a good woman, a loving father. Do you think that is possible, Zee. Can you see your way to helping me. Lord, how could any woman resist, him there in her bed, lying so peaceful between her sheets, the blue comforter tucked beneath his chin, his blue eyes always filling with tears, and not a single complaint, not once a word about the pain she knows he's feeling, his lung, the doctor says, punctured clean through by a Federal's bullet, a fingertip shot away.

Mama, she says, I think I love him.

Lord help us, her mama says.

1882

She doesn't look forward to the visits from Frank and Annie. In his tight suit with the black bow tie, the pin-striped trousers, the shiny boots, Frank talks like a schoolteacher, puffing his big cigar and looking at her as if amused with something, as if he finds her stupid, comical. And how, he asks, is the little mama. Annie glides through the doorway as if pretending to be a swan. She is a plump woman with large hands and feet, given to the wearing of pearly brooches above her commodious breast and many thick rattling crinolines beneath her bell-shaped skirts. Hello, Zerelda-dear, she says. It's *so* good to see you again. Frank sits in the rocker, creaking and puffing, in his schoolteacher's tight collar.

We been through hell and high water, Jesse says. Frank's the only man in the world I trust. He'll never betray me, Zee, not Frank, not for any sum of money. I don't know why you don't like him better.

She tries to. She tries to make conversation with him. And what, she asks him, pouring hot coffee into the delicate cup, do you think will ever become of the Indians? The subject interests her. It is a topic of interest in the East, she has noted, as well as in the West. The Easterner's point of view, she has observed, differs sharply from that of the Westerner. Is there room for all the tribes in the Indian Territory? Is it right that they should all be moved there—and can they really be guaranteed permanent asylum anywhere. Grant's policy was perhaps radical, though idealistic to be sure, but what will a man like Arthur do with the mess Hayes left. Frank has no opinions. He quotes her Shakespeare—he *says* it's Shakespeare. He reckons things will work out. He puffs his cigar, sips his coffee. Maybe, he says to Jesse, you and me'd best step into the other room. Ladies, will you excuse us for a moment.

Have you ever heard, Annie says, leaning forward in her chair, what the Indians do with the white women they capture.

She has read accounts, has Annie, true-life accounts, and the things they say will make your blood boil. Savages. Why, it's ridiculous to even think that a wild Cheyenne such as them that raid in Kansas will ever turn Christian. They are savage through and through, and the only solution to the problem is to show them we won't stand for any more of their outrages.

At least she has an opinion. As for herself, why, listen, what if you *were* captured by a savage Cheyenne, Annie. What would you do. Be honest now.

What would I do! Fight tooth and nail for my freedom, of course. I'd not give in. I'd run. I'd escape.

Would you. Well. I think I might not. Not if my brave had enough passion in him. Not if he wanted me so badly that he couldn't bear the thought of life without me and would hold onto me whether I loved him in return or not.

Oh, certainly, Zee, but I don't think that's the way it is, at least not in the accounts I've read.

Accounts! Why you don't think a woman is going to speak of such pleasure when she's recaptured by her family, do you. Would you? No. You'd have to protect *their* honor, save their pride. Or else be treated as the lowest of the low. No, I don't place much faith in the accounts.

Really, Zee? Don't you.

She shakes her head. Little Jesse pulls at her skirt. Mayn't he please go in the room where his daddy and Uncle Frank are? Mary sits in the middle of the room, legs crossed in front of her, her rag doll, a present from Ma Zerelda, flat on its face being whipped vigorously. Indian children would be quiet, well-behaved, trained from an early age to do their share. The air in the dark tipi would be sweet and leathery, her brave's eyes dark brown and unflinching, his touch, as he draws her to him, gentle.

She hasn't wanted this return. Missouri, he tells her, is our home, but she's been happy in Tennessee, as happy, at any rate, as she has ever been since their marriage. The death of the twins brings him closer to her for a time, and he begins to take an interest in farming. Then it's: We must return to Missouri. It is time. I feel it in my bones. There's no use arguing. When he brings up his bones, she knows it's no use quarreling, he's made up his mind, he's got to go.

What surprises her is the feeling of warmth she has. The Mississippi seems to move with the same pace and thickness as her blood. She feels steady, calm. Perhaps, she thinks, it *is* right, this return of the family to Missouri. How white the rocks that rim the hills, how thick and swirling the snow-washed grass in the valleys, how stately the rows of willow and cottonwood along the creekbanks, bark shining in the late winter sunlight like fine silk stretched tight and brushed perfectly clean. Then, at last in St. Joseph, bold in the spring sun, she walks past the storefronts along Messanie Street. *Mrs. Howard. I am Mrs. Howard of Lafayette Street.*

The house on the hill commands a view of St. Joseph, the Missouri River, and all of Kansas beyond. Home, she thinks, yes, he's right this time. This is our home. A child will be born here. It is 1882. The world is not the same as when Jesse lies wounded in my father's house and talks so foolish of families. Because it wasn't possible then—even I must have known that it wasn't possible to live in peace, not for him nor for me, not then, not in those times.

Merchants smile pleasantly, offer assistance. They are not suspicious. Why should they be. We are at last living the life we have planned for ourselves. She tells him she is with child and he kisses her hand, clasps it almost with tenderness. Mr. and Mrs. Thomas Howard, of Lafayette Street, St. Joseph, Missouri.

But then he goes. He rides off alone, leaving before daybreak, returns in a week, two weeks, a month, she doesn't know. His mother sits in the rocker by the fire, the chair not moving, and talks to her of burdens and injustices while the children loll about on the floor, calm as dolls for a change, drawing stick figures on their slates.

Things get worse, the old woman says, waving her stump, before they get better. I raised them up to be good boys, my Frank and my Jesse. They never gave me heartache such as my Susan did. They are gentlemen. I raised them up to be gentlemen. But they have no peace, while Susan, who has shamed her mother and her brothers more than once, prospers in Texas with that scoundrel Parmer. Lord a-mercy.

In the middle of March the chill winds give way to warm breezes from the south and the rain falls like mist. When the gray has gone, she takes the children to the river. We'll have a picnic, she tells them, with Aunt Annie and your cousin Bob. But the river's high and muddy, the banks thick with briars and silt. Annie sees a snake. And so they have their picnic lunch in the yard of the house on the hill. We can see the river anyway, says Annie. Who needs to be close to it.

When Jesse comes back it is the eve of April and the Ford boys come with him. Well, he says, you're swelling up just fine, but she's in no mood for sweet talk. She needs love and knows there's no getting it from him, not anymore, not ever, though it breaks her heart to think it. Where is she to get it, if not from her husband. She looks at her children and they seem not hers, some other woman's, and the child within her might be rock. She remembers, she tries to imagine the moments when his touch thrilled, his glance warmed. There was a gentleness, a tenderness. It was trust, she remembers, trust that we had. When, now, might that have been.

What do you think, Annie asks, of that Charley Ford.

Not at all, she says. I don't think of him at all.

Have you noticed the way he looks at me? Zee, he gives me the shivers.

Stop ogling him. Stop flirting with him, Annie.

Zee! You're one to talk.

They sit in the straight chairs by the south window, the dark curtains drawn back, the morning sun streaming through the panes. It is a warmth, she thinks, but not the warmth I need. She has lost that warmth, just when she believed she had it back, lost it as sure as she has lost her youth. When she hears the gun, she thinks it is the sound of her soul breaking loose from its skin. She closes her eyes, a girl again in old Missouri, Missouri before the war, waking to the sound of the mourning dove, the footsteps of her father, birds, so many of them, singing in the trees, beautiful, something fine and beautiful, her mother calling, Zee! Zee! and now the sun lighting up everything, Jesse her cousin, her lover, on his way to pay her a secret visit, him just a boy trying to look like a man by strapping that big pistol around his waist and letting the fuzz above his sweet boy's lips stay, blonding in the sunshine, curling ever so slightly at the corners of his mouth, where the cheeks soften and the chin drops like it wants speech, a tongue and mouth of its own. What has happened. What in God's name has happened. Zerelda, they're calling her name, but isn't it his mother they want and not his wife. It's always somebody, Shepherds or Hiteses or Cumminses or Liddils or Ryans, who could keep track of them, these mean-eyed men with their guns and their grins, their matted hair, their small teeth. Pleased to meet you, Ma'am. She is sure. How does he know, her blue-eyed Jesse, who he can trust. This one, no. This one, yes. And Frank, Frank forever.

What has happened. A gunshot or a slamming door. Jesse doesn't slam a door, leaves a room quietly, enters in silence. He is there or he is not and in either case you think that is the way it always will be, his presence all one with his absence, eternal his comings and goings. And so it is not like him, she thinks, rising from her chair, to go so noisily. Perhaps it is thunder. Perhaps nothing at all, her soul, her bursting heart, her wild imagination, her unsettled mind.

Charley Ford, what have you done.

No. It's Bob that's done it. Bob, my brother Bob Ford. Yonder he goes.

Zerelda, you mustn't look.

He seems to embrace the wall, her Jesse, the red coming on the back of his head like another set of lips that she might more conveniently kiss while the other pair, those pale thin ones she remembers always drawn tight like stays, squeeze against the skin of the room. Oh, she'll look, all right. She sees him lying there, for sure not wanting her, wanting no one to hold him back, a secret and safe, you bet, her Mr. Howard, gone for good.

THE HISTORY OF FRANK JAMES

What a day, the heat murder. He stands alongside the water cooler in the back of the store, one hand on the glass, and Jesus even that glass is warm.

Are you Mr. James.

The same, in the flesh.

I was told you might have shoes to fit me.

Might. Warm, ain't it.

Oh, yes.

He reckons he can fit her all right. She's been bestowed as average a foot as he has seen. Why, she might have been made by a store, ordered from a catalog.

You wasn't never one of the James Boys, was you.

She looks him hard in the eye, grinning, her mouth bent like a toe. He nods his head in the affirmative.

You mean you are the brother to Jesse James.

Yes'm. Though he is dead these several years, victim of a assassin's bullet, I survive.

My. And now you are a honest man.

Always was.

He sells to her high-top boots, last year's, the heels tapered like a cowpuncher's. She is legion, and the men, the unwashed farmboys with pale weedy mustaches and size eleven feet, their fathers, slightly smaller versions, never far behind, all want to know the same thing. He might open a museum, put himself on display. Why not. Don't his dear mother sell rocks from the creekbed, call them pebbles from her Jesse's grave. And Zee, she who at the funeral is so certain her Jesse's legs and arms have been cut off for somebody's souvenirs, wax ones stuck on in their place, that she cries like all get out to rip open the coffin just so she can inspect them, this same Zee is peddling everything her departed husband ever touched, guns to underwear. Why hold out. Shoes? Why, he might sooner sell himself, toes first, then a foot, a finger.

Well, he's about to give out, that's all there is to it, nothing to look forward to but a stroll across the street and around the square in the shimmery heat, the little meal from the dinner pail, a afternoon in the store in this starched collar, this shirt sticking to his skin, these tight oxfords. Who wouldn't begin to get a little restless, answer me that.

And Annie says, Frank, what's the matter.

Pass the meat.

She circles around him, hovers, now offering a basket of biscuits, now vinegar-soaked greens. Supper is the worst time. Robbie stares. Chew your food, Annie tells the boy, but he seems to prefer letting it soak to nothing in his mouth.

Could be worse, sure. Look at them Youngers locked up in Minnesota. Jesse dead. Stiles and Clell Miller and Wells dead. He begins to think the dead are better off. But then he remembers Belle Starr, wonders what ever become of her. There was a live one for you.

We could visit Zee, Annie says. Kansas City might be nice this time of year.

She's down in the Territory, that's where Belle is, riding wild through the canebrakes. Them deep eyes. Hands strapping on the gunbelt, long fingers quick as bees aimed for nectar.

Or we could visit Mother Samuel. When was the last time you wrote to your mother, Frank.

That boy staring at him.

Annie, why is that boy looking at me that way.

The boy picks a piece of salt pork from his greens, sucks it into his mouth, swallows it without a chew.

I'm going out.

Why, Frank. Where?

Where my own family don't stare at me.

It has seemed a good spot to locate, Vernon County, halfway between Kansas City and the Territory, on the edge of the old Burnt District, plenty of strong feeling for the bushwhackers. After the burning of the town of Nevada by the federals, it is built up again almost overnight. That is the kind of spirit Frank James admires. He is forty-three years old though, and wonders what he is to make of himself. Memories, he's got the memories, but what count are they.

Could be worse, he reckons. Out back he has a row of young maples and two mature elms, only one of them blighted.

But listen here. What if the whole point is the adventure, and this life here, this dull and decent life no life a-tall. Oh, who's he trying to kid. Let's get this straight. Remember the gnats, the horseflies around the campfire. The fear of the posses. Who will betray you. Who can you trust. There is Bob Ford, just a youth, taking Jesse like he was swatting a fly. You get to dreaming of them after a while, them traitors sneaking up on you, ready to plug you or slip a blade into you. Even now, listening to the wind in the trees outside his window, he has a lot of trouble getting to sleep. Annie, he calls, Annie. I'm in bad shape. I'm hearing things. She sleeps right on, breathing to beat the band.

June, he says, mounting his big roan, we are going for a ride.

Plenty of light left, these the longest days of the year. They always are, in his remembering, long days, the roads dusty and the birds chirruping, and here comes a snake, black and thick, swift from beneath a stone. After a while it is the moon making the light, enough to glaze the leaves, make softer the white of the rocks along the roadside. He can ride all night, ride for the Territory. Belle, he'll say, here I am. She won't know him at first. He's older, his head losing hold on its hair, his once dark mustache spattered with gray. The war has been over and done with for twenty-one years. May be it is time to stop the fighting. He remembers, bringing June to an easy canter, Charley Quantrill. There's a man for you, fighting until the end. If Charley Quantrill lived beyond the war though, what would have become of him. Wouldn't life have eaten him up, same as the rest of us.

Answer him that, will you.

Morning.
Morning.
Feeling better today?
Feeling all right.
You was looking poorly last night.
I'm all right.
You have to ride a long ways?
Yep. Where's the boy. Still asleep.
Now—
Wake him up. It's time he was awake.
It's time you got to the store. That's what I think.
You wake that boy up.
Don't forget your dinner pail.
Annie.
You tend to your business, Frank James. I'll tend to mine.
And just what is my business in this house. Tell me that.

Your business is selling shoes. Selling shoes. And you're going to be late if you keep fooling around here, worrying about what don't concern you.

I'm going.

Go then.

He walks to work, up Cedar Street. Other streets are named Cherry, Walnut, Oak, Elm, Ash. There is a Washington Street. A Main Street. His is Cedar Street. A modest neighborhood, his house small but on a spacious lot. On the other side of town a hospital is building, a state hospital for the insane. To the south one finds artesian wells. Plans are afoot to promote these waters, make a spa of Nevada, Missouri. On the northside stand several fine mansions. Judge Stratton's, Dr. Churchell's. The Hotel Mitchell on Cherry Street, a stone's throw from Moore's Opera House. Fine churches. A handsome courthouse. Strong jail.

Yep, a man would do well to cast his lot with this town. Someone with a little horse sense might do okay for himself. A fellow could raise a family here.

He tips his hat at the ladies. Do they blush? He believes so. A little color, just a touch, in their cheeks. In the store they present their feet. Shoe me, dear. Fit me, please, Mr. James. What if he touches her, there, just so, say, ain't that fine now, Dearie.

No, he is polite. A calm, reasonable man. A gentleman. Takes his dinner in the back of the store, sitting on the footstool, a broad lace-trimmed napkin spread across his lap.

Frank, what is it like to be a famous outlaw.

No, they don't ask. They think it natural that he should come to their town and settle down. They know their way is best. You are one of us, they tell him. Here's your shoehorn. Your hymnbook. To your heart's content, sell and sing. That is what we do in Vernon County.

Annie, he says, I'm a desperate man.

Frank, she says, I'm not going to listen to any more of that talk. How many times—oh, go to sleep.

Can't.

You'll be sorry in the morning.

I'm sorry now.

Go to sleep then.

Belle wouldn't ever tell him to go to sleep. Down there in the Territory, she knows what's bothering him.

Frank, look who's come calling.

He sits in his parlor, troubling nobody, shades drawn, a Sunday afternoon in July, just about to sleep, she knows how hard a time of it he has sleeping, why don't she let him be.

Frank, it's your mother. Down from Kearney.

He knows where she lives. It's Belle he's been dreaming of. Frank, she says, come this way. Leads him past Cole and Jesse, inside the cave, a light place, and she says to him, Sing. I want you to sing for me. And he don't know what in hell to sing.

Might as well wake up.

Son, his mother says, I'm weary.

Waves her right arm, that stump, and sits in the big rocker, sighing and rustling, her feet beneath the thick black skirt not quite touching the floor. Little feet. About a size five, he reckons.

Son, it's a long life. Why don't my time come.

Aw, Mama.

Mother Zerelda, would you care for a slice of melon.

Sometimes he thinks he might talk to her. Mama, he'll say, I have got troubles. Nothing's right. Nothing's enough. Once I had something, but now, well, I just don't know. Ten years ago, before Northfield—

Don't you talk to me about Northfield, Franklin James.

Aw, Mama.

I had enough of that Northfield.

Mama, it's how to live. That's what I want to know. Seems like nobody never taught me how to live. For a while it didn't much matter. Maybe I was young. Maybe I was just ignorant.

Your daddy was a preacher, a man of the Lord. He was not a Catholic, but a Baptist, and he had a way of making you forgive him. It is a pity you did not know him better before he run off to California.

What would he have said to me.

What he said to me, Son, was, I'll send for you, Zerelda. Don't you worry. You'll be hearing from me. You take care of them children now. What he would have said to you, Franklin, I cannot with certainty say. I feel it would have been important. He was a man who did not waste words. He seldom spoke save to tell somebody how to live. He had the last word on that subject, did Robert James, that reverend son of a bitch that was your father, running off and leaving me with three small children and a prayer book. Brings me out here to Missouri, a young bride scarcely a woman who don't even remember her catechism, gets me with one child after the other, you the first, Franklin, and then he lights out for California, promising to write, send money. Ups and dies in Sacramento.

No, he'll not talk to her.

Yes, she says, I will have a small slice of melon.

What brings you down to Vernon County, Mama.

I'm aiming to die. I'm weary.

Annie, bring me some of that melon too.

Reuben Samuel will not miss me. You can bet your boots on that. Might as well live with a chair. A chamber pot.

Mother Samuel!

A spittoon.

Aw, Mama.

You all excuse me. I'll go get the melon.

Surely.

Surely.

Robert James was flesh and blood, Son. I can't say the same of Dr. Samuel. A ghost in his time.

How've you been, Mama.

Sits there straight as a nail and weeps like a baby. I can't do a thing with him. It's drove me to despair, Son.

Well. Is he sick.

Spite, that's what it is. I had enough. Let me die in peace.

Now, what kind of talk is that. Is that what you come all that way to tell me.

Yes, it is.

Well now.

A grown man of mature years. Hand him a ear of corn and he weeps.

Say what's bothering him?

Don't say a word.

Take his meals regular?

Buttermilk and cornbread's all he wants.

But he eats that.

So fast you'd think he was going to choke to death. He'll die of cornbread stuck in his windpipe. Him that the federals couldn't kill by hanging.

Here's the melon, Annie says. It's real sweet.

Thank you, his mother says. I don't require a fork.

Nor I, says Frank, tucking the napkin into his shirtfront. Annie's given him a sizeable portion, and he heaves into it, holding onto the rind with his right hand, into the palm of his left carefully spitting the seeds.

My, says Annie, you two eat like birds. Let me get you some more.

She leaves the room, and then his mother, a black seed sliding from the corner of her mouth, whispers to him: This house is a disgrace. Don't she ever clean it!

It's August. It's hot. He waves a palmetto fan through the heavy air. Summer seems to have stalled. My Lord, the store, the store! Who wouldn't tire of them cartons, the dust, the gray walls, the abominable tile, polished slick, the thick and oaken door, the clacking feet across that creaking floor. Evenings, he keeps in form, firing rapidly into the creekbank. He rides. Give him a good horse, a long-flanked loose-limbed Indian pony, and he'll ride and ride. Jesse dead, Frank says I give up. Try me. Let me hear the array of charges against me. Put me away, if need be. But he has not imagined this kind of freedom. This deadly safety.

Two weeks before school is to start, he catches the boy with a book. Trash, he's sure.

What have you got there, boy.

Nothin.

Let me see.

Ain't nothin.

He snatches the book and the boy runs. Let him go. Can't catch him anyway, not anymore, not in a footrace.

The book is of the sort he's known it would be: *The Border Bandits, An Authentic and Thrilling History of the Noted Outlaws Jesse and Frank James, and Their Bands of Highwaymen*. Jesse was bold, it says here, Frank cunning. And look here. "Many improbable and romantic incidents have been credited to these noted brothers by sensational writers; so many dashing escapades and hairbreadth escapes attributed to them, which they never dreamed of, that thinking people, expecially in the East, have begun, almost, to regard the James Boys as a myth, and their deeds as creations of sensational dreamers...." And so on. Can you beat that.

Annie, he says, where do you reckon he come across this one. She blushes.

Why, I don't know, Frank.

Like hell. You give it to him, didn't you.

She stops her rocking, her knitting, looks him hard in the eye, her face dead white now.

What if I did.

He stomps his foot on the carpet and the dust rises around his boot slow and wavery like heat itself.

A passel of lies, he says. A tissue of deceit.

She commences to rock. Back of her through the window he can see the sinking sun the other side of the blighted elm. Leaves drop before his very eyes, months before their time. In the middle of the tree, perched on a branch close to the trunk, his cheek pressed against the bark, the boy stares, pointing at him as though aiming a pistol.

I'm getting out, he says to Annie. I had enough. I'm going.

On a dashing escapade, Annie presumes. After his Belle Starr, she supposes.

Let her guess.

Who's that?

Hello, Mama. It's me. It's Franklin.

Franklin, she says, is in Vernon County.

Mama!

He's rode hard all evening, dust thick on his face, and it's a black night all right, but she might recognize her son, her firstborn boy. He knocks again. Go away, he hears, the voice distant, from another room, and he knows there's no persuading her, there's nothing but to get back to Kearney and check in at the hotel. At the desk he signs B. J. Woodson, Nashville, Tennessee.

Why, hello, Frank, the clerk says. Whyn't you stay out at your mama's?

The room's small, yellow gardenias printed onto the wallpaper all in a line, one line after the other. It's damp and the bed smells of something rank, sweat maybe, if he's lucky. Sunk deep in the mattress and wishing for a breeze, all tired out from a long day's ride, he shuts his eyes and there she stands, Belle Starr, close enough to touch, a big grin on her face, one hand on the butt of her snug-holstered Colt, the other extended towards him.

Jesse, she says.

Jesse. Hell, he ain't Jesse. It's Frank, he wants her to know, and ever bit as good as Jesse. Some say better. The cunning one, some say, the smart brother, the brains of the outfit. She stands there and grins. He's sure glad this is a dream.

In the morning he finds his mother tending the grave. She stoops and draws up handfuls of pebbles from a tin bucket and sprinkles those pebbles around the headstone.

Are you deaf, Mama, as well as blind.

He dismounts, walks up to her. It's me, Mama. Franklin.

So I see. Lift that bucket up here for me. Don't like to be stooping.

He picks it up, pretty damn heavy, you'd be surprised. The little stones, white and smooth and flat, shine in the morning sun.

You carry this all the way from the crick, Mama?

That's where the best ones are.

Little heavy for you to be hauling all that way.

No one else to do it. They won't buy them unless they find

them hear the marker. Somebody's got to haul them up.

Expecting a crowd today.

It's August, ain't it.

Dr. Samuel sits in the corner of the front room, his hands folded neatly across his lap. Sunlight shines across his bare feet. He wears a black frock coat with sharp-pointed lapels and a white shirt with a celluloid collar that dangles, half-fastened.

Dressing him ain't so easy, she says, only this one hand. Can't get shoes on his feet. He won't do nothing for himself. Won't even answer when spoke to.

He's old, that's what Frank reckons.

Not as old as I am.

He hears what sounds at first like a whisper, thinks Dr. Samuel is about to speak, but then sees the tears in the old man's eyes, the mouth clamped shut. After all, he thinks, that ain't my father. My father's dead and buried in California. I seen the grave.

Still, he bears the man no ill will. Never did him harm, stood by his mother all these years. Those feet look like about a seven, he'd guess, small for a man, the toes turning under, long, almost, as fingers.

He's greatly reduced, his mother says, from what he was.

You want me to, I'll put his shoes on for him.

When visitors come, his mother, a leather pouch strapped around her waist, leads the way to the grave. He was a good boy, he hears her begin, a decent man that loved and respected his mother. He is sorely missed by all that knew him. The visitors stand in a circle around the grave while she talks, her head held high, her hand outstretched. Then—he sees it all from the window, keeping himself hidden behind the curtain—one of the visitors, a gray-bearded man in a silk top hat, kneels, picks up a pebble, turns it over a few times in his hand, with a smile pockets the stone, drops a coin into the leather pouch. Others follow suit, some with bills.

Across the room Dr. Samuel makes his whispering sound and the tears are flowing.

What do you want with me, Frank asks. I've put your shoes on you. What else can I do. Aw, stop your crying.

Now Dr. Samuel raises one hand. He raises it slowly, as though it were very heavy, but the palm of it flashes pink like a little flame.

Maybe, Frank thinks, I can talk to him. Maybe I can tell him my troubles, ask him what is a man to do.

Dr. Samuel closes his fist and shakes it in the air and his mouth opens. Quit that now.

They're coming. Run quick. Out the back. Go!

Run from a bunch of sightseers! He's not going anywhere. Not until he's good and ready. Doc, he says, leaning forward in his chair and peeking again out the window, we got all the time in the world. Keep calm and steady. Trust Frank James to get us through.

She brings the sightseers no closer than the porch. In the house, he hears her telling them, there's nothing you'd care to see. They shake their heads, doubters all, but then scatter. Back inside, his mother tosses the pouch onto the table, sits down to calculate the take.

THE LIBERATION OF THE YOUNGERS

Cole, Jim says, do you think you've been properly reformed?

Yep, says Cole, and that's all I want to say on the subject.

In the driver's seat of the buckboard Cole sits straight and stiff as a telegraph pole, his long legs stuck out over the edge of the footrest as though his knees will not bend. It's summer and they are on a tree-lined dusty road somewhere in the middle of Minnesota, the sky more white than blue.

What I want to know, says Cole, is how we're going to make this next sale.

Next sale!

All right. First sale. All the more reason to give it some considering.

I don't think we're going to to make it.

That's no way to think. We'll make it.

There are things I'd rather be doing.

Rather be back in prison, I suppose. Serve another twenty-five years.

That's the trouble with Cole. Always turning your words against you. How can you talk to a man like that. You can't, but the solemn truth of the matter is that, other than that team of glue-bait, weak-kneed Jesse the bay and half-blind Frank the dappled mare, there's no one else. Just good old brother Cole, old poker face.

Jim, Cole has said to him, know what I'm going to do when that pardon comes through.

What's that, Cole.

Why, I'm going to travel all over this country, from California to New York. And you know what I'm going to do?

I sure don't, Cole

I'm not going on a sightseeing tour. No, sir. I don't aim to have a good time.

Hell, no.

What I aim to do is lecture.

Is there money in lecturing, Cole?

Don't care about the money. What I care about is the youth of this great nation. The state of their soul. I want them to know that crime don't pay.

Well, the pardon comes through all right, with parole, and that parole says, You boys ain't leaving the state of Minnesota. Twenty-five years ain't enough. You get you a job right here in the state of your transgression. You got to pay *us* back. What's more, no lecturing nobody. No displaying yourselves, boys, for the sake of a profit. Find yourself a honest job like the rest of us. Else it's back in jail for the Youngers.

I didn't want to lecture anyway, Cole says. What right have I got.

The air's thick with gnats. It's hot, the sky too close for comfort. Jim's jaw, shot to pieces twenty-five years ago at Northfield, starts to bothering him. Always acts up, he's noticed, when the sky's like this, a slow ache, a throbbing until the thunderheads come and the air starts to smell of rain. Cole hums, then lets the words out, almost whispering them: *Come to the church in the wildwood, the little brown church in the dell*... and the words trigger something, a big sound, not an explosion so much as a splash, like a flood might sound, a wall of water striking hard against the side of a barn. He's sitting at the end of a long table, before him a silver plate, shiny and empty. The table is so long he can scarce make out who's sitting at the other end. It's his mother all right.

Her plate is full, the steam from hot ears of corn rising thick as fog. She won't pass him nothing. He looks around. It's a small room, too small for such a long table, the walls pressing in close. He hears clanking from somewhere. The doorknob comes off in his hand, a Bowie knife. Through the window he sees his father coming in from the fields. No, it's Cole, atop a horse, why it's just a colt, legs spindly and bent in at the knees. Cole's big feet drag in the dirt.

Gnats get into his ears. He's back then, swatting, poking. Ahead he sees the farmhouse set back off the road, its tin roof dull as the sky, off to one side a windmill, a few low-slung outbuildings, wood weathered to gray. The barn leans eastward, towards the furrowed fields, the line of trees beyond. A mule stands still, very still, between the house and the windmill.

Cole, he says, I don't think this looks like a good prospect.

Reckon we'll give her a try.

He tugs the reins.

Whoa up there, Jesse. Ho, Frank.

Steps onto the porch and pretty near falls through, the wood rotted out. Next to the door a hound glances up, then lays his head back down, thumping his tail twice.

Anybody home, Cole hollers, rapping on the open door.

Flies buzz in that dark room. The man taps his long yellowed nails on the table top, and the woman sits in the corner, hunched in a straight chair, her eyes closed, lips working as if she chewed something tough. You can see the barn through the window. A string of blackbirds has alighted on the top of the roof, big starlings, plump as pigeons.

A man's got to die, Cole says.

That is a fact, says the man. There's no denying that.

Yessir, it's the one thing in this life a fellow can count on.

Ain't that the godawful truth.

Many's the time Jim here and me—and my brother Bob who is no longer with us—why, we laid in the arms of death and did not know if we was ever going to get up on our own two feet again. Ain't that right, Jim.

Sure is.

And I'd say to Jim here, Jim, I'd say, if we was to up and die at this moment, if this hour was to be our last, do you think there'd be a soul on this earth remember us.

Ain't you boys got no mother somewhere? the woman asks.

Yes'm, says Cole. We sure used to. Bless her soul, released from the cares of this world.

Thought so. Most everone does.

Yes'm, but you see, we wasn't in a position to keep in touch in those days.

Jim's laugh is controllable at first, and he's not concerned, the conversation, the sales pitch, can continue, but then it's awful and he can't stop. *We wasn't in a position to keep in touch*—Christ, that Cole!

Is he going to be all right, the woman asks.

What is it, the man asks, you boys is selling anyway.

Memorials, says Cole.

Memorials. Well now.

Jim looks away, about to die, out the window at the barn. More starlings than ever, huddled up along the peak of the roof like people, squat and sleek, their dull beaks crooked as noses. Cole talks, but from far off. It's as though Cole's in another room even though there he sits, the farmer next to him rapping the table, skull cocked to one side, a fly strolling across his smooth and wide forehead. Something emerges from the woman's mouth, a wad of tobacco he sees, but it is as though a small dark bird, one of those starlings maybe, too long trapped deep in her throat, has leapt for freedom and, before its fall to the floor, tried for flight.

You stink, the woman says. You boys smell like the devil.

Mama, you hush now. You listen to what Mr. Younger here has to say.

That ain't no Younger. I seen pictures of them Youngers. Them that is sitting there ain't no Youngers.

Sorry, boys, the farmer says. Don't you pay her no mind. You go right ahead. She ain't been right in the head ever since—

But Cole rises, and oh my, here we go.

Madam, he says, and he throws his shoulders back and clears his throat and runs his fingers across that shining head where once the hair has grown thick and dark. Madam, I stand here before you, Cole Younger. In my time I have rode with the best of them. I have hid in the canebrakes while all around me the hounds leaped and sniffed and never found me nor harmed a hair on my head. I slew the jayhawkers with Captain Quantrill at Lawrence and lived to ride with General Jo Shelby. I taught Bloody Bill Anderson the rebel yell. Whipped Jesse James to within a inch of his life. Loved Belle Starr until she knew the meaning of the word. Younger? Madam, I am Younger clean through. Madam, you look at me, you look at Coleman Younger in the flesh.

And this yer, the farmer says, you say is your brother Jim.

I don't believe a word of it, the woman says. And I don't want none of your memorials neither. You boys come to the wrong place, I reckon. You must think we're a pack of fools, a story like that. Now git outen here.

The farmer shrugs his shoulders, stands.

Cole bows, first to the lady, then to the gentleman.

Thank you for your time, he says. We can find the door.

I hope so, the woman says. Seein's it's right behind you.

For a long time after that, Cole is silent. That's okay by Jim. He watches the trees. What, he wonders, are their names. There's a oak, there's a maple. But all the others, some with smooth trunks, some with branches slim as fingers, leaves frail as grass, what might they be. Strange country all right. Should have never come up here. Who'd ever dream they'd still be here, twenty-five years after climbing down from that train in Mankato. Who'd dream they'd still be alive, them that rode under the black flag with Quantrill, all these years Quantrill dead, killed on the run at the end of the war.

No mountains, no hills, a country of sudden lakes and strange trees.

They wasn't very hospitable, was they, Cole says. Southerners too. That's what hurts the most. Wouldn't have been like that in the old days. We'd a been received with open arms.

Yes, says Jim, but we wouldn't a been selling no tombstones.

Nope. That makes a difference, don't it. You're right, Jim. That seems to make a difference. These farmers, they just think on the here and now. They're just getting by, making no provision for the future.

You wanting to go back?

Go back. Back where?

Why, to Saint Paul. Where else can we go.

West to the Dakotas. South as far as Ioway. North, why, north all the way to Canada. The northwoods country. The big lakes. The tall pines.

Hell fire! Nowhere.

Grand Rapids. Duluth. Plenty of places.

Suppose we're going to sell tombstones to lumberjacks.

We might consider it.

Why you suppose that woman asked about our mother.

Cole shrugs his shoulders and Jim sees his mama in the gesture.

There she is, inside Cole looking out at the rear end of a scrawny horse. Dead these thirty-some-odd years, but quick to plague him with his faults, his no-good ways, her chin shaking with her anger, her little eyes shining like they was just minted, but then she's sinking back in her pillows with a sigh and a shrug as though nothing in the world matters, nothing's worth getting worked up about, no son of hers will ever amount to a hill of beans, why get troubled, why get upset.

Mama was always proud of us, Cole says.

She fed us when we was hungry.

She hid us when we was chased.

She raised us up from little babies.

She was a sainted woman.

Bless her heart, she did her best.

It was good enough. It was just fine.

I got no complaints. She left us to our ways.

She knew what was what.

Cole, let's drink to Mama.

Cole lapses into his silence, his grand silence, tightens his grip on the reins, grits his brand new teeth.

Why not drink to her, Cole.

Don't talk to me about drinking.

Hell, Cole.

Drinking's the devil to pay. I'm aiming to lecture on that someday.

Listen here. Do you believe Mama would buy one of them damn tombstones for one of us, was we dead and her alive?

I do. I know it. I feel the truth of it in my heart.

You was always her favorite. Her darling Cole.

I loved my mama and I respected her.

I'll drink to that.

It is a weakness.

I'm weak. Just now I'm feeling real weak. My head aches. I'm not at home in this country.

Just remember. We are on the job.

Some job. In the middle of Minnesota selling tombstones and the damn company don't even trust us with a sample to show. I tell you it's a joke. Somebody's laughing at us somewhere. Here. Have a swig. Wet your whistle.

Just a swallow. No more'n that. My throat's dry, all this dust.

So dusty you'd think it was Texas. It ain't though.

Forgive me, Mama, Cole says, and he turns the bottle up. Poison, he says. I'm going to lecture on it someday.

She's staring at them, standing in the shade of a squat little tree, looking at them with big clear eyes, a slender one she is, her bare feet white as all daylight sticking out from beneath a black and shining skirt. Back of her the house looks like it comes with her, a white house fresh-painted, porch swept clean, alongside it a pump that looks as though it has just been polished, and beneath the spigot a bucket of clear, clear water.

Jim grabs the reins. Not here, he says.

The trees lean in towards the road all in a line, Frank and Jesse towards the trees. For miles it is that way, the sun up ahead of them more pink than red through the haze, not moving an inch, you'd swear, hanging there just above the tree-tops as though at the end of its rope. Through the trees you see more trees, dark with slick trunks, and there is a sound in the branches of the trees that is a little like crickets in the jackoaks of Missouri only he's sure it's not anything he's heard before, too steady, too shrill.

Minnesota frogs, says Cole. We'll be coming to a lake soon.

Jim sees it already, aglimmering off in the north, white and smooth, trees all the way to the edge of it, and he can smell the water, the wet leaves, the mud.

Are you of a mind to bathe, Cole asks, passing the whisky.

Up close the water's brown and still and smells like well-boiled coffee. They wade in up to the waist, the water cool and the lakebottom soft and slippery.

Ain't deep, is it.

Naw. Think we could go right to the middle of it and the water not even chin high.

A shallow son of a bitch.

A broad spot in a low crick.

Jim remarks the whiteness of Cole's belly, the way it curves into the surface of the brown water. Where, though, is that bottle of whisky.

I got it right here, Cole says. Letting the water cool it.

Don't let that water *in* it.

Think I'm a fool. I got my finger plugging it.

And Cole starts to sing:

> *Rescue the perishing, care for the dying,*
> *Snatch them in pity from sin and the grave—*

Come on, Jim. Sing with me:

> *Touched by a loving heart, wakened by kindness,*
> *Chords that are broken will vibrate once more.*

He sings low, off key, and Jim's not tempted to join in, don't know the words anyway. Only song he can sing is Dixie, and he's forgot most of that. I'll just listen, he says, but then Cole stops. I'll be damn, he says. Where'd it go. I've lost that little son of a bitch, Jim. Gone, it's gone into the murky deeps. And he waves both hands in the air like a fool, leaving brother Jim, good brother Jim, dependable brother Jim, to dive for it, which he, also like a fool, swiftly does. Only I know I'm a fool, he thinks as he lets the water come up over him, a good feeling that quick shock going under, that's why I'm doing it. He swims with his eyes open though he can't see a thing, just Cole's legs and the lower half of that white belly, until he pushes himself deeper and can touch as well as see the bottom. He cups his hands then and strokes the water, swims until his lungs are bursting, towards the darker water in the middle of the lake, the light far above him, flimsy and pale, and no sound at all. Comes up for air and down he goes again, this time to the shallow water, the lost bottle afloat not six feet from where Cole's standing, a big grin on his face.

Jim Younger saves the day. Whoo-boy!

Someday, he says to Cole, Jim Younger's going down and he's not coming back up.

Cole laughs, turns splashing for the shore.

Come on. You got more of that hooch stashed away in the wagon. I'll bet my life on it.

Nope. That was the last of it. Not another drop.

Don't you lie to me, Jim. I know there's more.

Cole heads straight for the buckboard, not even bothering with his clothes. What's in this trunk, he says, pointing, naked as a jaybird.

Hymnbooks.

The hell you say.

Cole touches him on the shoulder, a hand cold as the devil.

Keep your hands off of me.

I want you to open up that trunk. Are you going to open up that trunk?

Just keep your hands off of me, Brother.

I'm not desperate. I'd like another sip, that's all. Bathing works up a man's thirst.

You sure got simple needs, don't you, Cole.

I know you got more whisky in that trunk.

When Jim comes down, he's down, he's way down. He looks up

at the stars and sees them moving towards him. Cole, snoring in his bedroll, is no help, no presence to speak of. If he could weep, he would, but damn it he's got no sorrow left. Woman, he wants to say, I love you. But she won't hear him. It's a rough time, seeing her back there beneath the tree, them clear eyes and sweet hands. He didn't want to see her. She's no business of his.

He thinks about the water. That was a sweetness too. That diving into a dark quiet place. But he can't stay there any more than he can tell his love. He's a coward. That's the long and the short of it. He can't go after what he wants. Prison suits him just fine, yes, it's his kind of place, it might have been designed for him. He sits down at the long table, the plate shining before him and empty as sin. Then in comes Quantrill. Hello, boy, Quantrill says. If you got a weapon and a mount you can join up with me. Before that his father's brought home in a wagon, that shadow, that distant man, shot dead by the federals. He remembers his mama's grief as if it was his own. So this, he thinks, is to be my purpose. To redress grievances. Quantrill wears a red shirt, fringed at the shoulders, and leather britches. I'm going to help you, he says to Jim, avenge the death of your father. Ride with me. All you need's weapon and mount.

The nights are longest. Can't ever be sure where he is, who's watching, who's out there in the trees. He keeps the knife beneath his blanket, the rifle in the wagon a few steps away. The world's all wrong. How can anybody live in it, everywhere you go something waiting for you and meaning you harm. It's no justice, Quantrill says, unless you make it. Dead is Quantrill, chased out of the barn he's hid in and shot in the back.

In the morning they find the road again. Cole is sullen. He has not, he reports, slept well. Jesse and Frank plod along, flies lighting on their haunches. It warms up early, the morning sky going gray fast, the wind dying and the mosquitoes thick. Seems to be a sparse settled region. Reminds you a little of the Indian Territory, though he reckons that place has changed considerable since they was there last. In those days you could ride and ride and not catch sight of house nor cabin. No railroad and the towns few and far between, west of the crosstimbers nothing but red dirt, sand hills, ravines. A few Cheyenne camps. Along the cattle trails, a few run-down dugouts that call themselves trading posts.

Cole, if we was allowed to depart this state, where'd you go.

Missouri.

Back there everybody's dead.

Everywhere everybody's dead. Missouri's home.

I might go to the Territory.

Belle Starr's dead.

There's other reasons for going to a place.

Not to that one. It's all settled now. Ain't you heard. They opened up all that territory. Did it while we was hindered from partaking.

In the distance now is a house, a white frame farmhouse, trim as you please.

There, says Cole. A pretty sight, if I ever see one. Look at that barn. A silo. A milkhouse. A wagon shed. This is it, Jim. I feel it in my bones.

You do the talking, Cole.

Just back me up, brother. And say, this time let's not tell them we're Youngers. Say we're Howards. Say I'm Howard, you're Jackson.

You're the boss, Mr. Howard.

That way we let the product stand on its own merits.

The finest memorial available

Right, Mr. Jackson. I feel good fortune coming our way. Let's do this one for Mama. Carry us home, Jess. Gidyup, Frank.

Cole shakes the reins and that team, headed for surefire paydirt, lurches forward.

CHARLEY FORD BETRAYED

Charley Ford remembers how Jesse brings the dark coat of the horse to a fine sheen, stroking slow and easy like he means never to stop. The smell of the straw, the aroma of the horses, take the chill off the air. This horse, Jesse says, is a miracle. He'll carry you anywhere. He's strong and he's got heart. He'll run like the wind when another'd give up the ghost. You want to ride him sometime, Charley, you can. Fall asleep on this horse, he'll get you back home. A horse like this don't come along but once in a lifetime. I'm telling you, he'll see you through!

What is it that you call that horse, Jesse?

I call him Shake. Short for Shakespeare.

A lot of good his Shakespeare done him. No more than his sweet Zee with her small hands and narrow tapered fingers, than his mama Zerelda Samuel with her dark prune of a mouth, her stumped right arm shining in its pinned sleeve like a present. And smart brother Frank, mustachioed and scented, the words of the other Shakespeare always on the tip of his tongue, don't matter at all when Bob Ford shoots and Jesse jumps, falls back into the wall and then down in a wink to the floor. Now you're done for, Charley thinks, hearing the hurried footsteps of the women in the hall, the rapid breathing, the walls humming, the sunlight slanting through the drawn curtains like a wedge of pure light come from nowhere, from the window itself. Where are you going to hide now, Jesse James. What name are you going to find for yourself, how are you going to make yourself disguised, how mount your huge horse and ride him home. Now you're done for, Jesse James!

Charley has let Bob talk him into this tour. Their first stop is Saint Louis. East, Bob says, is the best direction. It is where the big audiences are.

The opera house is near the levee. You can smell the water, a brown smell, and hear it too, that little lapping, water washing over the egg-shaped rocks easy as you please. Lord, let him have that peace, just for a while, a spell of calm.

In the saloon the man says:

Well, well, so these are the famous Fords.

He's a tall one, his face straight up and down with a pink little chin dimpled in the middle, smooth-shaved but with the burnsides growing clear down off his jaws and onto the long neck, curly and thick, swooping back up and meeting beneath a hooked nose. Bob grins his horse-face grin, shaking the man's hand like it might otherwise get away from him, says, I am the slayer of Jesse James. And this yer's my brother Charley that assisted.

How-do, boys. I am Jesse James.

Are you now. Haw, haw.

May be you can help me portray the character, get the feeling for the man, you might say, behind the mask.

You bet. We're your men. You got the right boys for the job.

Jesse wears a beard. It's dark and full and his eyes are blue.

That right. Well—

Small hands. Small feet.

Charley is a keen observer, ain't he!

Jesse had two little children, a boy, a girl. Was married to a perty wife.

Don't forget his mama, Charley. Old one-arm Zerelda!

We got her in the cast already, boys. The mama and the wife, played by two of the finest actors ever trod the boards, John Jessup and Billy Gashade.

And Frank James. Don't forget brother Frank.

We got Frank.

Jesse always carries a pistol. On that day he wore two. A Colt and a Smith & Wesson. But he laid them pistols down. Frank was nowhere around.

I did not shoot, says Charley. There wasn't no need.

How I killed him was like this. I step forward, me between him and the laid-down pistols, then I draw and aim and fire. He has turned and sees me. He is facing me when I get him.

There wasn't no need, says Charley, for me to shoot too.

You boys are like I pictured you. A pleasure. A rare pleasure.

We done our duty. That is the way we was brung up, Mr. Bunnell.

They are in a long room with a lot of men standing around. Charley wonders what are the men looking at. What do they see to stare at. Is it his long fingers, the nails unclipped. His little neck, slender as a wrist. His puckered lips, his thinning hair. He admires Bob's swagger. Bob steps into a room and he is in the crowd right away, his back slapped, hand shook. *Howdy, boys.* But he, Charley, can smile and strut like the dickens and still they stare, then look away like they was sick at the sight of him. This time they look at him a long time, their big faces lit by the oil lamps at either end of the bar.

Howdy, boys. I am Bob Ford, slayer of Jesse James.

They look at Bob then. No backslapping. He hears them breathing. It is as though a lot of hounds slept on a porch, breathing deep. He remembers how the boy, holding onto the hand of his mama, comes up on him sudden, looks him in the eye, knows him, and it's just like he's looking at himself, not at the son of Jesse James at all, himself, little Charley. What a look! You run along and leave me alone, boy. This is Saint Louie, not Saint Joe.

The men turn away. No boy stands beside them pointing. Charley, you are a damn fool. Get aholt of yourself.

They sit at a table scarce the breadth of a sombrero, their knees pressing together. The place smells rank, like the river gone sour, a yellow smell.

What are we going to do, he wants to know.

Whatever Bunnell tells us, that's what. We don't need to know nothing.

I'd like to know something, Bob.

You don't have to, Charley. Don't get in a sweat. Always worrying about what you don't need to worry about. Gee-zus.

Sure, Charley thinks. Why is it then that the sky feels so heavy, that the wind smells rottener than a chicken coup, that the trees make such ugly sounds, all winter using their roots like tongues. *Jesse James, Jesse James.* The wind whines the name, stings like sand in his eyes until he can't see nothing, and then the coldness sets in, a chill enters. In the center of him: a hole, a cave, a hideout, not warm, and once you're in there's no getting out. He circles it. He has an idea Jesse James is in there watching for him.

They walk along the levee, the two of them alone. The stones nearest the water are damp and slick, green around the edges. Stuck firm in the ground, they can't be pulled loose. You'd need a pick. The riverboats are big as buildings, their paddlewheels turning slow, foaming the brown water.

I would like, Charley says, to be someplace else.

I'd like, says Bob, to be in Paris, France.

I'd like to be someone else. Maybe if I was to walk out into that water, I'd come out on the other side someone else.

Over there is Illinois. Chicago's that way. Walk into that water, most likely get whopped back of the head by one of them paddlewheels.

I'd be underneath the water.

Ain't it a fine evening.

It'd be dark and cool underneath the water.

Getting dark now, cooling down fast.

And quiet. Real still.

Chilly for June, breeze coming off the water.

I'd be someone else.

You'd be dead, Charley. That's what you'd be underneath the water.

New and clean.

Clean and dead. Lungs lined with mud.

I'd be beautiful, I think.

Like a log. A toad. A catfish.

I'd like to have another chance.

Looky here, says Bob. The Lord is looking after us.

The women are tall, both of them taller than Bob and him. The hems of the long skirts glide across the floor, making a sound like the wind in leaves. Charley's love carries a parasol, sharp as a spike, beribboned at the handle. She has a clean scent with a bite to it, and when she turns at the top of the stairs, the light from below flickers in her eyes. Taking him by the wrist, she says, I am sick to death of this place.

It's a wide hallway, almost a room, but it doesn't go far. At the end of it stands a wall, a picture painted all the way across it and up and down it, gray-uniformed men, mounted, their horses with thick haunches and upraised heads, the sky behind spoiled by red and yellow flames. On either side of the painted wall is a white door in a bright blue jamb.

See you later, brother, says Bob. Sweet dreams!

The door closes with a quiet click, a little whoosh of air like a catching of the breath.

Jesse James is dead and I am the one that done it! When he hears it, he thinks yes, this has to be, Jesse James can hide hisself no longer, somebody has got to find him out and deliver him to his right destiny. There's a reward waiting for them that can do it. A fortune to follow. Now, says Bob. *Now,* he says, aiming. Jesse turns and starts to say something. It sounds like it might be, What do you want, or What have you got. He's grinning, is Jesse James, his teeth gray as gunpowder, his blue eyes for once not blinking, wide open even with that early-April sun streaming through the windows. Staying wide open, them clear blue eyes, until Bob leans down and shuts them up, just before the ladies come running in, screaming in spite of all their training not to, Zee's long skirt rattling like paper. *Charley Ford! What have you done!*

It was Bob done it. I swear, Zee.

She doesn't look at him again. She runs for her Jesse, and then the boy, his little sister close behind him, comes in and takes a long hard look at his dead daddy. Let's go, Charley, says Bob. They go, Bob even then starting to shout, *I killed Jesse James! Jesse James is dead!* And outside, the still bare trees stretching across the road branches frail as cobwebs, all Charley can think is, Ain't it a shame.

If you was in his place and him in yours, Bob says, you think he would of thought twice before he took aim? Hell, no. The idea, Charley, is to stay alive.

That was death.

Listen. Think of it this way. It is the same as when the leaves fall off of the trees.

Jesse James is a leaf.

Think of it that way.

We shot a leaf off of a tree.

That is about the size of it, brother. Only remember, *I* shot it.

He's feeling warm. You'd think it was a summer day, August, and no shade in sight. Standing next to him, pistol in hand, Bob looks stiff as a stick of furniture, his face going yellow in the light, shiny with sweat. From out in the dark a voice yells out, hoarse and deep:

Okay, boys. Let's go through it once more.

From across the stable Jesse glances at Charley, not stopping his stroking. The horse's eyes are closed, his dark coat glistening in the lantern light. Jesse speaks almost in a whisper.

It's a long life, ain't it, Charley. Sometimes I don't know what keeps us going. I think of my mama, how she has suffered, a son killed, a arm blown off, and I think to myself what is the use of it all. Do you ever think such thoughts?

He does. Yes, indeed.

Jesse's voice rises, and the horse's eyelids lift up, just enough to show off the crescent of a dark eye shining like the devil, but then, Jesse stroking and stroking, the lid eases down again.

Charley, Jesse says. Will you join me in a prayer?

I ain't a religious man, Jesse.

But he can no sooner spit out the words than he's on his knees.

Lord, Jesse prays, who am I and what am I for? Remove the motes from out of my eyes so that I might see.

Charley's love thinks at first that he is Bob.

No, he tells her, I am Charley.

You look like Bob.

We are brothers.

Honey, it don't matter.

155

I have a sister. A widow. Martha is her name.

I have a brother name of Billy.

We was always close, Bob and Martha and me. We played in the fields. First it was Virginia, then Missouri. We laid down in the dirt in the corn rows. The sky looked closer then, but the crows stayed far away. I'm a hawk, Bob would say. I'm a butterfly, says Martha. And I, says I, I am a ear of that corn. The crows sound like hounds and the dust is cool and soft. I thought I could smell the clouds, but maybe it was the corn stalks. There wasn't any snakes around. We would have heard them. The flies was big and black.

Her dark skirt and white blouse, folded in a neat stack beneath the lacier garments she wears closest to her skin, look solid as a step at the end of the bed. He sits steady in a straight-back oak chair, the rungs pressing at his spine, his long feet crossed and tucked back under the seat. His hands, he sees, have got up in front of him, and he brings them down quick and pockets them deep.

I always thought my brother was better than me, he says. I never liked it when people mistook me for him, him for me.

Is that right.

Mama favored me best, next to Martha. Charley, she says, Charley, you are a pretty child. You have got such long eyelashes. I believe the Lord intended you for a girl, Martha for a boy.

I loved my daddy best, she says. He held me on his lap and said, You are my sweetheart, honey, and patted my hair. His hands were big but soft. Not a tooth in his head, but you never see a sweeter smile. Mama loved Billy best.

He remembers the way she comes towards him, the sound of her voice as real as it can be. What is your name, he wants to know, her hands making his skin feel like skin you'd want the feel of, and she says, Glory. My name is Glory Gashade. My daddy named me Glory Hallelujah. You are a hymn, child, in praise of the Lord, he told me, but your brother Billy is the devil to pay.

Glory Hallelujah. World without end, Amen, Amen.

That's just what my daddy use to say.

Bunnell sits in a squat little chair, his long legs stretched out in front of him.

I am Jesse James. Who are you?

We are the Ford boys, robbers and marauders.

Are you mean? Are you cunning?

Bob draws his pistol. I could kill my brother here if I had to. If I wanted to.

And I can trust you?

You can place your trust in me. I will give you my loyalty in return.

And you, Charley.

Yes, sir. We are your men.

We was—were—born to rob and kill.

Outlaws is our middle name.

I am Jesse James. I am called the Bandit King. In truth I am a decent man, an honorable man, a good father, a dutiful husband.

In glides a small man in buckled slippers and a satin dressing gown, the famous Billy Gashade, his head shaped like a turnip, broad and smooth at the top and pointed at the chin, a little tuft of sandy-colored hair way back on the crown combed flat straight across so as to meet a redder fringe that stops just short of the ears. He grins, and he's got the whitest set of teeth you ever see, like they was painted, his lips flat and bluish. I beg your pardon, he says.

Ah, Zee, says Bunnell, rising. Zee, these gentlemen are the Ford boys, Bob and Charley. Gentlemen, my wife Zerelda.

Gashade curtsies, extends his hand. The best in the business,

Bunnell has said. Trained by the brilliant George Christie. We're fortunate in having him. Charley sees little likeness to Glory. Billy is round where she is lean, hard where she is soft, Billy's hands cold, rough, hers warm and smooth. Only in the eyes, clear and gray-green, does he see a sign of Glory, but it is so sure a sign that, kissing Billy's hand, he shivers and turns away and will not look into his eyes again.

Pleased, I'm sure, says Bob.

Bob lies stretched out on top of the bar. There's nobody else around. Charley looks back of the bar to be sure—nothing but bottles and mugs and jiggers, lined up on a thick pine shelf. A little light's coming through the windows, a square of it atop Bob's belly, where he's got his hands clasped so that the big fake jewels in his rings flash like little fires. *Brother, our time has come.*

The hands fit together, the thick fingers one across the other, the roof, the steeple. They look like they are breathing, each nail a face with a mouth to suck in the air, each mouth curving to make the same blank grin. I might have done it, Charley thinks. He shot first, but I might have done it. I needed longer to aim, that's all. That's the difference between him and me. One brother that shoots, one that aims.

In Jesse James's house the shades are drawn. Charley sits in the corner of the big front room, little Jess on his lap. You look like your daddy, he tells the boy. The spittin image.

My mama and daddy are cousins, the boy says.

Zee takes him away. Come along, Tom, she says. Bedtime for you. She lifts the boy to her arms, though he is big for his age, already grown up to her shoulders. Her dress is the color of pumpkins and she moves in it like it was nothing but light, through the wide doorway into the still darker rooms in the back of the house. Jesse clears his throat. Bob wipes his forehead with a ragged bandana.

Is it too dark in here, boys? asks Jesse. He wears a string tie and his wide suspenders bunch up his shirt around the shoulder holster. How much does he know? Plenty. You don't dare think when he's around. He hears. He laughs at you, slaps you on the back, his palm hard as hickory. Charley, he says. You are one ugly son of a bitch. Frank steps up right behind him, says:

The baby beats the nurse. Athwart goes all decorum. Shakespeare.

You don't say.

I do.

Maybe Charley here don't know what you mean.

Maybe so. Maybe not.

Bob laughs. The James boys, he says. Who'd ever think I'd be riding with the Jameses. Charley, ain't this the life.

Frank slouches in the rocker, the big book open on his lap, his eyes shut, his mustache, brown as all get-out, twitching like it was a muscle.

Jesse passes the cigars. Charley remembers the hands, the pink stub on the right hand smooth as the tip of a nose.

Boys, I feel like you two are almost family.

The room's small, the bed hard and narrow. The scratching sound he figures is a tree branch scraping against the window. His eyes adjust quick to the dark, always have, shadows no cause for concern. It's a long way from Saint Joe, the breadth of Missouri. They've buried Jesse beneath the coffee-bean tree in his mother's yard in Kearney. It's a big shade tree out a ways from the house, but close enough so's she can keep an eye on the spot. He sees her sitting on the porch in a rocker, her half-arm tight at her side like it was strapped there, the other hanging still with its hand in her lap. Maybe she rocks, maybe she don't. She's remembering. She's looking.

When Glory presses against him, soft and warm, it is just like they are one person. Glory Charley Ford Hallelujah. Mama, look at your baby girl, all growed up in Glory. Glory, get your Charley with child.

How much, he asks, do I owe you.

How much do you think I am worth.

A whole lot. A fortune. A wagonload of gold. A million. All the banks in Missouri. The Mississippi River.

Make it a hundred. I got nothing against blood money.

Bob jams his pistol into its holster. Damn, he says. This is getting old.

Bunnell strolls towards them, working his jaws so that his burnsides twitch like they was trying to reach across his face, cover up that plump mouth and dimpled chin. He says:

Howdy, boys. You have heard of me. I am Jesse James.

And Bob says, That's your cue, Charley.

We want—

We—

To join up with your band, whispers Bob.

Yes. We want to join up with your band. We are outlaws—

At heart.

We are outlaws at heart.

Outlaws, says Bob, is our middle name.

It is in our blood.

We was—were—born onto lawless.

Ness. Lawless-ness.

Yes. Onto Lawless-ness we was born.

We want to belong to your band.

Bunnell crosses in front of them, arms folded across his chest. Daddy. He looks like my daddy. About to scold me for something I done wrong. His boots heavy, the planks beneath them squeaking from the strain of that weight, he looks like he thinks he is talking to the sky. Then he stops, turns, swift as a lizard, and sees you, points his finger and aims his eyes. *Leave the cornfield to the crows. Don't let me catch you there again, hear? You are meant to protect your sister, not favor her with your attentions.*

Wake up, Bob, It's day.
Who's that? Charley?
The same.
Whewee—wasn't that a night!
Get kicked out of bed?
Naw, I just wore out, Charley. Imagine that. Me, wore out.
Bob sits up, spins around, jumps down from the bar.
Where is everybody? Hell, Charley, ain't nobody else up yet.
I don't know where they went to.
They're sleeping.
What are we going to do. I can't sleep.
I'm awake. Once my eyes are open, I'm awake.
I didn't sleep much, but I can't sleep. It's day to me.
They walk down to the levee. There's nobody around, the shades drawn in the red brick buildings, paddlewheelers still and quiet in the silvery water, across the water the dark line of land that is Illinois, the sky laying above it, a dim and heavy haze, no breeze to speak of, the sun just a rumor, maybe it's back there, maybe not. For sure taking its time. With Glory, it's *World without end, Amen!* You're no one and nowhere, forget about where you come from and when you have to be someplace else, your fingertips atingling and blood athrobbing, before your eyes a sight to beat

all: your soul fleshed out, its skin all lit up in grace and beauty, shining like it's made out of eyes. Hers.

Brother, where are we. Why are the streets empty.

My pleasure, says Gashade, and then, stepping forward, just beyond Bunnell, facing the darkness of the empty opera house, he says, I do not trust the looks of these strange men. Something about them tells me, Beware, and a chill has set upon me, as if Death, pale and tall and swift, has paid a call, left its card. I have a fearful foreboding. I shudder to think what may happen. I begin to see that my most terrible imaginings, my most loathsome nightmares, all too easily can come true. Lord, help me to remain calm, not to reveal the darkness I feel so mercilously fanning outwards from my heart, thicker than blood.

We are not supposed to hear that, right? Bob asks.

Right, says Bunnell. We remain frozen while she speaks.

Cue! Thicker than blood—that's your cue, simpleton!

Bunnell shoots Bob an angry look, then smiles big, offering Gashade his arm, and says:

We'll be seeing a lot of these boys, Zee.

Fine, says Gashade. I will look forward to their company.

Hasta la vista, boys!

So long, Mr. Howard.

Goodbye, Mrs. Howard.

Oh, but who are these strangers? Why do I feel I've seen them before!

Tossing about on the fainting couch in Jesse's front room, he hears through the thin walls a cry. It's Zee, he knows, saying the passion she's feeling. He's cold and sick at heart, his legs bent and stiff, aching like crazy, his feet numb. It's dark, but he can see Bob across the room sitting in Jesse's chair, sound asleep, just back of him the window with its trees and stars hid from view. Something's plaguing him. This restlessness ain't natural. He's used to sleeping, to long dreams of seeking and running, restless dreams, sure, but dreamed while sleeping. His legs ache and he can't stretch them out. In the trees beyond the window the crickets whine. Bob whistles in his sleep, his head bent at a sharp angle, his hands resting in his lap, just touching the brim of his white stetson. Through the walls, Zee James cries out. *Oh, Jesse, ohhh....*

This was all a long time ago, when Charley Ford knew his soul was through with him and, save the death of Jesse James, there wasn't nothing to look forward to but daybreak, the flesh and its mean desire.

BILLY GASHADE AND GLORY

> *This song it was made*
> *By Billy Gashade...*

A great opportunity has at last come the way of Billy Gashade. Sitting at his dressing table, the thick and beribboned crinoline billowing from his corseted waist, he holds the telegram before him, reads and reads it again: *New melodrama opening. Jesse James Betrayed. Want you for the grieving widow. Promise of a long run, agreeable profits for all concerned. Notify the undersigned as soon as convenient within 48 hours of receipt. Bunnell. Olive Street. Saint Louis, Missouri.*

Convenient? He'll wire his acceptance posthaste. Out of the crinoline, loosed from the stays, he sees himself already in Saint Louis, once again walking the streets of that great western city, strolling along the levee of the river of rivers. The women, why there's nothing like a western woman, so artlessly guileful, graceful in mirth and in grief abandoned. There was a woman once that wore a pistol strapped around the waist of her velvet gown, in one breath recited the poetry of Lord Byron, in the next spoke to the virtues of Jesse James. The Wild West? Railroaded, corralled. Custer dead, the Sioux subdued. This is 1882, son.

Comes a knock on the door.

Please enter.

John Jessup, red in the face, breathing heavily, steps into the room.

Billy, it is your mama. She says she's dying. She says John, go get Billy. Says she's got last words and she wants you to hear them!

How has he come to this. Ain't it strange, ain't it a little mad. A young man, a boy, he watches for the posters that announce the time of the minstrels. He languishes in the stuffy parlor amidst crystal figurine and plaster statuette. Gilt-edged volumes rest tight in their shelves and smell like flesh as it begins to sweat. Dark walls. Heavy drapes brushing the floor. A scratching, a scurrying, as if small animals live in the walls, something smaller than mice that might ease through one of the narrow cracks near the baseboard and proceed to do harm.

Father clears his throat, strikes a match on his heel. Mother's gown swishes. She smells like a gardenia, her small feet in boots of smooth leather, edging from the hem of her silks as she steps into the room.

Brown streets, bleak skies. He would be elsewhere, but where? The puddled roads of Cincinnati lead only to the knobbed hills of Ohio and Indiana. Across the Ohio River is Kentucky, more trees, more hills, gray bluffs giving way to grayer mountains. Strange people live in that direction, people who, according to Mother, want nothing to do with the civilized world, live little better than savages in rude cabins on rocky mountainsides. Why? They have no place else to go to. They are unsuited, they are ignorant, they are degenerate.

There is a better world, she tells him, holding him to her smooth bosom, the dark silk soft as skin. No, Father says, the world ain't as we would like it to be. It don't yield to our fantasies, Son. We must take it as we find it. The toughest amongst us survive. Pity the rest.

Slender, frail, sickly, Billy lies in his parents' bed, covered with heavy quilts and scratchy blankets, his mother's hand on his forehead. No minstrel show for him this year! His father in the tall-back chair close to the wall, near the door, breathes heavily, rubbing his palms on his trouserlegs. It is not that Father would not come closer. Papa merely shows restraint. I must go, he says finally, standing, his pink hand already turning the doorknob. There's work to do. Mother does not appear to notice when the door downstairs is slammed. He loves you, she says. You must understand that your father loves you. You are his son, his only son.

The other son, who would have been a year younger than Billy, dies before taking his first step. He is named Christopher George and is buried, in the graveyard of the Presbyterian Church, Our Dearly Beloved Son Sorely Missed. After that come daughters, four in rapid succession, Esther, Emma, Mary Elizabeth, Alice. Mary Elizabeth comes to resemble her mother, with the same flashing brown eyes, the pale hands, the languorous graceful movements. Esther looks like Papa, has his long parabolic nose, his cinnamon-colored and peanut-shaped eyes, his ponderous gait. The others— Emma of the auburn hair, little Alice of the dark ringlets, the lace collars, the flushed cheeks—seem early to find their own moulds. Emma sits in the parlor in the dim light of dusk and strums melodies on the dulcimer Father has made for her. Alice takes up embroidery, stitches elaborate designs on the hems of her drab skirts, whorls of violet or lavender, indigo or rose-red, crescents of robin's egg blue.

Billy reads novels in the shadows. Come here, Billy, says Esther. I want to show you something. She whispers through a crack in the door. Papa is at the bank, of course, and Mother braves ice, in the sleigh calling on an ill friend. It is the day after Christmas and snow lies smooth among the fragile trees, not melting, hardened by icy winds from the north, the roads silvering in the pale sun. The holidays! All the morning he has listened, from his father's big chair in the parlor, to the footsteps and occasional laughter of his sisters above him. Chores done, he has chosen a volume from the flesh-smelling shelves, opening the glass carefully. Shall it be

Walter Scott or Fenimore Cooper? He passes over the commentaries on Calvin, on Knox, the concordances and the prayer guides. Scott it shall be. *The Heart of Midlothian*.

Come here, Billy, I want to show you something.

Open the door and she's gone. An empty hallway, dark and cold. But the sound of her footsteps on the stairs, and then: Oh, no. You'll not see. It's too late now. But it isn't. She's brought him forth from Jeanie Deans and he will not go back until he has seen what she has to show him, damn her soul. He swiftly ascends the stairs. Esther, let me in. What is it I'm to see. He puts his ear to the door. If there is motion, why then it is brought off quietly. He can hear nothing. He listens hard. *Boo!* It is Esther. She has come up behind him, clapped him on the shoulder. A strong grip.

It isn't fair!

Shh... it is too, you'll see. First you have to say the password.

I don't know the password.

That's why I'm here. It's—

And she whispers in his ear a word he thinks sounds like *Damascus*.

Damascus! he says. Then he hears the laughter behind the door, but it opens and Esther pushes him into the room. In spite of the dark, he sees the reason for it. They have hung blankets back of the curtains.

Damascus! Esther says, and suddenly the candles are lit, the sisters all in a row before him, Emma, Mary Elizabeth, and Alice, each with a candle, Esther remaining by his side, her fingers clasping his frail arm.

Happy Birthday! Alice cries.

Happy Birthday, the others echo.

It's not his birthday. His fourteenth birthday has been duly noted, adequately celebrated, three months previous, in the fall of the past year, streamers hung from the ceiling, a cake consumed, a Bible presented. Now they laugh, these sisters of his. Esther wears his father's long black frockcoat, his stovepipe hat, stands tall in his boots, his vest, his cravat expertly tied.

You don't look like him, he tells her, lying. You don't look anything like him.

I don't *mean* to. I mean to look like myself and nobody else.

You look foolish.

I feel fine.

Father will be angry if he finds out.

I don't care!

Billy, says Emma. We have made up a play.

Yes, says Alice. And we want you to be in it.

We want you to be—

Hush! says Esther. I'm the one to tell.

Tell then.

All right. We have made up a play.

He knows that.

We told him that.

Hush! Sit down, Alice. Not another word, Emma.

I haven't said anything, Esther.

I know, Mary Elizabeth. You're the smartest one.

I get to be the grandmother. That's why I'm smart.

Esther folds her arms across her chest. She paces in the center of the room. The others sit still, watching her. They are children, after all. Dutiful. Obedient. Properly chastised. Mary Elizabeth smiles at him, the very image of his mother, though only for an instant before once again she looks at Esther. Alice frowns with great severity, and Emma closes her eyes, her hands clasped in her lap. In the candlelight her auburn hair shines beautifully. It looks like fire, he thinks, all that wonderful color in motion. His own hair, grown long and brushed diligently, would look like that. Feverish, his skin slick with sweat and his mother beside him laying another blanket on, he remembers Emma's hair in that candlelit room, the volume and motion of it, the calm sheen, the pure flame of it. *Emma! Pray for me, Emma! Strum a melody for me on your dulcimer. No more blankets, Mother!*

She sleeps. He sits beside the bed. Her face is calm and white. Across from him Esther, sobbing softly, dabs at her eyes with a lace-edged handkerchief. Her grief, he feels, comes late, but is altogether proper. He will save his weeping for later, only proper, though were he woman! Ah, put a brave face on it, Billy Gashade. Sit still, stoic in your hard chair. Emma will not come, not all the way from Saint Louis, nor Mary Elizabeth from her safe tomb next to Father in Ohio. Only Esther, Esther of Washington Heights, late of Long Island, large Esther, Mrs. George Brooks, matronly in her thick skirts, her powerful stays, her hats tall and turbanlike.

Where is Glory? Bring me my Glory.
She's out in Missouri, Mama.
Where's Billy then?
Right here, Mama. I'm Billy. And there's your Esther.
Where's my Glory?
She's far away, Mama.
Is that Esther?
Yes, Mama.
Billy?
Yes, Mama.
And your father?
He's dead, Mama.
Thank goodness. Are you sure?
Yes'm.
It is a comfort to know that. A small comfort.
Esther weeps into the handkerchief. He remarks the length of

her fingers, the breadth of her wrists, remembers her in her father's frockcoat frowning, pacing the floor of that upstairs bedroom, dark with the shutters locked, the heavy drapes closed. She strikes a match, lights a candle, another, hands one to him, lights another, hands one to Emma. *You are the bearers of the light.*

His mother rests. Esther, her eyes dry now, stands, walks slowly to the window, her figured silk rustling. She pulls back the drapes, and the dim winter light flickers, makes a long rectangle that crosses the floor and touches the foot of the bed.

What is that?

Can she have felt the light? No, it is something else, a complaint pushing into her dreams, some old intrusion. How is it that we grow to this. Father leads him through the crowded sidewalks of Cincinnati, his bootheels sounding on the damp planks like pain itself, the routine pain of our lives, a steady thudding followed by brief stillness, and all around you the others, the tall and burnsided men, the derbied and the mustachioed, the sheltered and the decorated bodies stepping, thudding, scraping through their lives. Melodrama of grief, dreary routine of remorse! Billy, Father says, it is a hard world that awaits you. He knows, does Billy, he knows. His mother's better world lies out there beyond the streetlamps, throbbing in its soft globe. Hasn't he been walking towards it all his life? And is this where she has led him, is this what she has had in mind all along? Yes, yes.

Billy, Esther says, returning to the bedside opposite him, do you remember how it was. Do you remember the long days, Emma and her dulcimer, Mary Elizabeth and her grace, little Alice's red cheeks when she ran in from the cold, asking for Papa. Papa, she called, here's sweet Alice asking for you.

Hush. She's sleeping.

She's sleeping. She won't be disturbed, dear brother, by what I have to say to you.

You've said it, Esther. What you have to say, you've said before. I've heard you. I've listened long and well.

You've not listened. You've not heard. You hear your own voices.

Nonetheless I hear.

When I speak to you, it's as though you are elsewhere.

I hear you.

I say again. Your father loves you.

He is dead.

His love is alive. It was a loving life Papa led.

You would believe it. It's his life he's given you. It's my life he wants.

That's not my voice you're hearing, Billy Gashade.

The voice of reason.

The voice of an actor. A minstrel's voice.

Let *her* speak. Let our mother speak her mind.

She can't speak, Billy.

I hear her.

She's silent. She's not awake.

She's eloquent. She's heartbreaking. It is her triumph!

When Mary Elizabeth died, she said, Pray for Billy's soul.

I heard.

I prayed.

I said Thank you.

And when Emma ran away, disgraced, Alice set the dulcimer on fire. She'll not be wanting it again, she said, not where she's going.

Alice wasn't always spiteful.

Emma wasn't always a whore.

Our Emma is a dancer, Sister.

I know what she is, what she has become.

You know, it seems to me, what you want to know.

Still I know it. I say it.

I hear it. Damascus, Sister. Our secret.

You can't blame me for what has happened to us, Billy. You can't blame me for your sorry state, for our Emma's fall.

I feel sorry for Alice, I regret the burning of the dulcimer. I blame no one.

Blame? What is this talk of blame?

His mother has spoken. Her eyes remain shut, but the lips have moved. I'm warm, she says. Who has covered me with these woollen blankets in the dead of summer? Is it you, Glory?

Glory isn't here, Mother. It is not spring yet, certainly not summer.

Is it Glory who is the whore?

Emma is a dancer.

Yes. And Billy a minstrel. Esther a wife, a mother. Lord help us!

I'm only myself, Mother, your Esther. Emma was Father's Glory.

I told him not to call her that. John, I said, she will have an inflated opinion of her worth. She is my Glory, he said. And there was Esther, yellowing in the corner, her hands stiff in her lap, dry, dry Esther, lost in an ill-lit room.

Mama. I am here. In *this* room. Your Esther is here, Mama.

And where is *he*, where is John Gashade.

Mama, Father is dead.

It's my husband I ask about.

Dead. Passed away. Gone from us these seven years.

Then he won't come?

He's gone to his reward.

Ah! Thank goodness. He wanted that so badly. Was it handsome?

Was what handsome, Mama?

The reward. Was it sufficient.

Oh, Mama. It's his *eternal* reward.

I hope it was big enough for him. He had such—cravings.

At any rate, he won't be coming.

I don't want to see him. Tell him I don't care to see him.

She opens her eyes then. Dark they are, dry and clear, astonishingly clear. Esther shoots him a quick glance. It means something—she never looks at him without meaning—but whether anger or pain or reproach he can't tell. It's a brief scrutiny, perhaps no more than that, and then she reaches for his mother, whose hand has arisen from beneath the blankets. It has hold of his wrist.

Bring my son to me. I want a word with him.

She is terribly lucid. How can it be so? Truly it is a miraculous recovery. Her cheeks flame up, her eyes moisten and dart about, her grip of his wrist so strong that he feels nothing in his hand and must beg her to release him.

My life, she says, has been long and hard. I have no regrets. I die a Christian. I will get what I deserve. It will be enough. It will be right. I never cared for my husband, but I did my duty by him. He was not at fault. He was not to my taste. Five children I bore him. Three survive. I have loved each as I have been able, and each has repaid me in kind. All my life I have wanted to love, I have had love in my heart to give. He did not want that love. There was no one to accept it the way I felt I could give it, and so I kept it to myself and grew unkind and solitary, no one to trust. Yet always was this love with me, it was my own, my hope and my despair, my pride, my shame. My own.

She looks at him, takes his hand again. This time she is gentle. Already her cheeks have paled, but there is warmth in her touch, light in her eyes. Her head might have no weight at all, so slight a mark does it make on the broad pillow. She is smaller than he has ever realized, frail as a flower. Lift her to the light and you would see through her.

Esther?

She's in the next room, Mother. You sent her away.

She resembles my husband. Have you noticed?

Yes.

He lost his teeth, one by one. In a month there was nothing left. No false teeth for him! I admired that. But he was much embittered and came to resent me. You are Billy, aren't you.

I'm your son. I'm Billy.

My how you've changed.

I grow older.

Father?

Your son.

Father will not come. Not for the world. He likes his boys best. Esther?

It's Billy.

Is she out of the room then?

Yes, Mama.

Can she hear what I'm saying?

The door's closed. You're whispering. I don't think she can hear you.

It seems to me I'm shouting. Well, listen to me, Son. I want you to do me a favor. Will you do your poor mother a favor?

Yes. What is it you want.

When I die—are you listening to me—when I die I want you to shut my eyes for me. Will you do that? I want no one else to do it. I want you to do it. Don't let *her* now, do you hear me. You do it yourself. Will you promise me?

I promise, Mother.

It is a great relief. Bless you.

I promise.

I did not relish the thought of *her* fiddling with my eyelids. It is a relief to know you will be the one.

I will be the one.

Bless you.

Thank you.

You are the very image of Father.

The Mississippi is as broad as he remembers it, as brown and as handsome, the levee a feverish blur of crate and deck, brick, boot, and parasol. He has traveled by rail, speed a necessity, but looks on the massive paddlewheelers—their boilers smoking, bows listless in the gentle lap of the water—with great admiration, a kind of envy.

Bunnell is sorry to hear about Mrs. Gashade.

The trunks of lavish gowns and crinolines are carried upstairs to his room by men whose bare shoulders shine with sweat.

Glory has been here, says John Jessup, asking for you.

Bunnell introduces the Ford brothers, who in the melodrama of Jesse James Betrayed are to play themselves. They have long hands and wear tight waistcoats and high-heeled boots.

I, says Bob Ford, am the slayer of Jesse James.

There wasn't no need, says Charley Ford, for me to shoot too.

Bunnell, a tall man with burnsides that cover his cheeks sleek as fur, announces that he himself means to play the role of the Bandit King. Frank James will be cast directly.

Glory, jeweled and satined, steps into his room as if the floor were made of gauze that a more careless woman might fall through. In that auburn hair surely resides the power of beauty itself. Sitting just opposite the faintly glowing light, the play of shadows across her face like spirits seeking shape, she holds her hands still in her lap, but for an instant he sees them move, stroke again the strings of the dulcimer, those same hands, the music the same, a chord he's heard all his life, as if, alive as trees, it quivers everywhere in the air.

Did you do as she asked, Billy?

She slept. She woke. Again she slept. When she woke, she did not speak except to call me Father, Esther Mother. This went on for days. I did not forget my promise, but the last sleep marked the last waking.

And so there was no need?

No need, Emma.

Then tomorrow I dance.

Tomorrow I take my womanliness to the stage.

I let my body move to the song my soul hears.

I wed myself to the martyred outlaw.

GLORY

Glory combs her auburn hair. Thick it is and aglow, she would swear, with its own light. She remembers her mother's tight curls, the ringlets dangling at neck and forehead, and how the mirror rises from the marble top of the dresser and the green bottles stand by the red, the squat by the slender, everywhere the fragrance of flower and the sound of hair combed to life, whispering its pleasure.

Behind her, Billy stands clutching his hat, a black bowler with a black ribbon wrapped around the base of the crown. In her mirror his face looks fuller, plumper than she knows it to be, and his eyes, always shining, the very shape and shade of Mother's eyes, shine now, surely making tears.

She told me, he says, to shut her eyes. You do it, Billy. I want nobody else to shut them for me but you.

You were her favorite, Billy. Her darling boy, her only son.

At the end she took me for her father, Esther for her mother.

Mama was no saint. She had her faults.

Lord knows! There was Papa.

Papa was one of them, yes.

Papa was a weakness of hers.

He abused her, Billy. He made a dishonest woman of her. She ought to have made her own way—

Oh, but she did. She had her way, her own life.

She served him, not herself. And he had no sense—that banker!

You were his Glory, Sister.

I forgive him for that. But not for Mama.

So you've said.

So I mean.

How easily she loses the sense of his words, hears only that long lament: love me, love me. And yet he does love me, she thinks as they walk together down the stairs. Billy loves me as his sister just as Father loved me as his Glory, sees me the self he wants for himself, my skin the skin of his soul. And when I dance, it is true: my skin is not my own, my blood beats in the veins of strangers, no one stranger than myself, my own hands so desirable that I would touch them and want their touch.

How still it is, how quiet. In the lobby, pale men sit deep in their dark armchairs, smoke rising from their faces, slower, darker air. Billy leads her through the room, his head held high, and then they are in the sunshine, arms entwined like lovers, before them landau and brougham and buckboard passing noisily on the red street. The air is remarkably clear, invisible but close. After all, the season is spring.

I always wondered what I would do, Billy says. Now I will see.

He looks dapper, somewhat like Daddy, she would say. He might be a banker out for a stroll, escaped from his cage for an afternoon, in those striped trousers, tight at the ankles, and that waistcoat snug as the corsets he wears when, a minstrel, he acts the melodramas.

A man approaches, separating himself from the crowd on the sidewalk. She cannot place him, but is certain that he knows her. He is dressed all in white, save his boots, which are black and narrow, hazed over with dust. Briskly, he steps up to them.

Billy! he says, lifting his straw hat. And to her: Ma'am.

Smiling, he shows her his teeth. They are surprisingly small, like children's teeth, and he shuts them up again quickly, as if his mouth were a jewel case. The lips, surrounded by the curling hairs of carefully trimmed burnsides, are plum-colored, smooth and full.

Glory, says Billy, may I present to you Mr. Bunnell. Mr. Bunnell, my sister Glory.

How-do, I'm sure.

Bunnell bows deep from the waist, a stiff bow, his right palm flat against his belly, left arm angled behind him as though to hide the hat he holds. She knows who he is all right. Bunnell. Of course. Billy's patron. Bunnell of Olive Street. The King of Melodrama, the minstrel prince. This the man who is giving Billy the opportunity to play in *Jesse James Betrayed*, first here in Saint Louis but then who knows whereall else. Chicago for sure, Billy says, his eyes glowing. Cleveland and Buffalo. Perhaps Cincinnati. I will be remembered in Cincinnati as the son of Lily Gashade, brother to Glory. But I will be unforgettable as the bride of the Bandit King, bereft and beautiful.

Oh, Billy. Whatever will become of you.

I've had the pleasure, Bunnell says, carefully replacing his straw hat, of observing you in performance, Miss Gashade. It was at the Pantheon, I believe. A fortnight or so ago. Admirable. In fact a treat. Talent—I said to myself—surely runs rampant in that family, don't it. How many other Gashades, I wondered, are trodding the boards. Are you legion, Miss Gashade, you and your brother Billy?

Oh, no, just the two of us.

Well, well, well. Ain't that a marvel.

There are other sisters, Billy says, but they are elsewhere.

Elsewhere indeed. What, she wonders, has become of *us*. Esther was present, Billy has reported to her, at their mother's deathbed, large, sad-eyed Esther in her rustling crinolines, her whalebone stays, her tight-laced boots. Mary Elizabeth is dead. Alice in disgrace in Philadelphia, wed to a Sheriff's man. And

Emma, she is Glory Gashade, her father's Glory Hallelujah. Play a tune for me on the dulcimer, Glory, and sing, such a sweet voice.

Sisters and brothers, says Bunnell. Ain't it a wonder.

She snaps open her parasol, the sun now very bright and warm. Ahead of them the courthouse looks so important, all portico and pediment, column and dome, it might be where the light comes from.

Say, I have got some folks I want you to meet.

He tugs on Billy's arm, and Billy hers. They pass Olive Street, then turn up Locust. Trees line the brick sidewalks. Handsome two-story homes at the edge of the walks rise like walls, solemn on their native stone, windows deep and dark as eyes, and beyond stand the steeples of the famous Saint Louis cathedrals, high sharp reminders of the bright sky and its hidden bundles of dark stormclouds. The sky, Billy says, will never stay in its place. Now he walks beside her, his gaze downwards, as if he must be certain of each brick, suspects the ground of treachery. Bunnell, looking at her, begins to whistle, the tune unrecognizable, perhaps something from the melodrama, a phrase from the overture. His mouth looks like an ear, those plum-color lips surely soft as lobes.

Could you dance to that, Miss Glory?

I can dance to most anything, Mr. Bunnell. I prefer fiddles.

At the Pantheon I admired you. And before that at the Grand.

I'm gratified.

Glory has danced all her life, says Billy. I remember—

Hush, Billy. We've had enough remembering.

We were children. You stood by my bed. I was sick, wrapped in wool blankets. It was as though I dreamed.

You did dream. I don't remember.

You danced. There was no music, but I heard the music you danced to. It was as though the fiddler sat at the foot of my bed.

A good fiddler, says Bunnell. There ain't nothing like a good fiddler.

But nobody was there. It was just you and me, Sister.

Maybe it was Esther. Maybe Mary Elizabeth.

Your body shone, each move a ray of light.

Beautiful, says Bunnell. Beautiful. I love a good dancer.

And I remember thinking: I am that dance. I am not my sister, but I am my sister's dance.

A lovely thought!

You always did have an imagination, Billy. I remember that.

I lay there: the dance. My fever had passed. A miracle, Mama said. Her palm was warm against my forehead. Father stood by her side, his hand on the bedstead, one finger tapping.

I don't remember that, Billy.

You were in another room.

Here we are. This is the place, folks.

What place, Glory wonders. Is there any other place than that house of memory with its dark halls and dank rooms, even in her own mind the shape of the world, what motion comes to. She remembers, Bunnell leading the way into another house, how Father places the dulcimer on her lap. You are the one, he whispers, with music in your soul. The dulcimer is curved, she thinks, like my own body. He has made it in my image, and the wood, walnut, he says—is smooth, almost, as skin. Emma, Esther says, Emma, what is he like, what do you think Father is really like. And Mother, for that matter. Mother bends over poor Billy, wrapping him in blankets. No minstrel show for you, she says. You are far too weak for that. And to her, to her Emma: a woman has a cross to bear. You may be your daddy's glory, but he has other glories. They live in the hills across the river in their damp cabins, pale in the shadows, straight as trees, your father's glories.

Bunnell guides her. It is almost a push. His hand against her back feels like a board, the butt end of a plank. This room that he's guided her into is small, with a high ceiling and a long window beside which has been set a big brass spittoon the shape of a gravy dish. Two men with small bright eyes the color of pecan shells sit by the window, identical broad-brimmed hats in their laps. One grins, one frowns. The expressions seem permanent, or at least put on some moments beforehand, as if before a mirror, and fixed firm in place. They look familiar, but she is sure that she has never seen them before, on stage or off. Something flashes, and she sees that the smiling one wears several rings, and that he is moving each hand slowly across his thighs, as if the better for the rings to catch the light.

The smiling one stands first, then the other, his hat falling to the floor.

Boys, Bunnell says, here's Billy Gashade and his sister Glory.

Charmed.

Pleased.

The boys bow low and long, their dark hair falling forward. Billy extends a hand.

These are the famous Ford boys.

I am Bob Ford, the smiling one says, slayer of Jesse James.

I am his brother, who was present at the time, Charley by name.

Bob takes Billy's hand, and Charley kneels, picks up his hat, then rises slowly and looks at her as if he expects her to step forward, do him violence.

She gives him her hand, which he takes and swiftly drops.

Bunnell laughs. Kiss a lady's hand, he says, when it is offered, son. And to her: Madam, you must forgive him. A country boy. A rustic. A farm lad from old Missouri. He means no affront.

The other one, Bob, one jaw swollen with tobacco, takes her hand and presses it to his lips so hard that it is like being kissed by a skull.

I regret what I done, Charley says.

Not me, says Bob. I got no regrets.

Well, well. Let's make ourself comforble, bygone be bygone. Learn today from yesterday, as my old daddy use to say.

That is good advice, Mr. Bunnell.

I know it, Bob. A wise man is a wonder, rare the fellow that speaks what he knows, blesséd he that hears and understands, curséd he that shuts his ear and sees not.

Thank the Lord for our agéd parents!

Sit down, please. Everybody make theirself at home.

Bunnell pulls cane-bottom chairs close together. The men stand until she is seated, then drop to their chairs like a shot, in unison.

Now, let's get down to business.

Bunnell shows her his little teeth again, briefly, and shuts up the lips. When he talks the lips curl over the teeth, the mouth held taut and the mustache going shivery on him. *Let's fool Billy*, Esther says. Let's play a trick on him. And so she slips into Father's frockcoat and paces the room, the hem of the long coat just above her boot tops. Glory, Glory, Esther calls out, pacing, where's Daddy's Glory.

Billy curtsies. Shyly smiles.

It is enough, Esther. It is enough.

Happy Birthday, Billy! We've made you a play.

Esther plays Father, Mary Elizabeth plays Grandmother. She plays Billy, Billy herself. The dulcimer lies silent on the sill. Billy dances, but he is not graceful. He nearly topples the candles, and finally she has to say, Stop. I hear our mother at the door.

The frowning man's cravat is tied inside-out, held fast with a ruby stickpin. He is thin, with a long neck and long hands, his scalp shiny beneath hair that seems somehow listless, or inclined at any rate to be elsewhere. His cheeks, clean-shaven, the color of old newsprint, are flat but sunk slightly like the palms of hands.

I mean to play myself, Bob Ford says. I know what I done.

It is what the public wants to see. It is what they will pay to see. I'm banking on it, boys. I'm banking on a long run. Then we go on tour. We take the show to every major city. *Jesse James Betrayed*. With the genuine parties on the stage.

Save Jesse James.

Ha, ha. I like a man with a sense of humor. Save Jesse James! Very good, Billy.

Who plays Jesse James?

Her frowning boy Charley has asked it, his lips scarcely moving. Show me a man who frowns, our mama has said, and I will show you a man at peace with himself. Grinners head straight for hell.

I mean, Bunnell says, to play that part myself.

Bob lets fly with a stream of tobacco juice that lights in the spittoon with a ringing sound.

That's a good one, he says, wiping the back of his hand across his mouth. Tell me another, ha-ha.

Why, I'm in earnest, Mr. Ford. I mean to take the part myself. I have qualifications, experience.

Hell, Charley says. Anybody can get shot.

Beg pardon, Mr. Bunnell. You want that part, why, you can have it. I meant to cast no aspersion.

I made up a song, says Billy. It goes like this:

> *Jesse James, Jesse James, there's no more of Jesse James,*
> *Robbing the banks and the trains ...*

I'm sorry. I've got no guitar. Glory once had a dulcimer, Father a fiddle.

Inspiring, Billy, inspiring.

I don't sing well.

But you got heart.

I need accompaniment. A fiddle can do a world of good. Alone, the human voice is weak, falters where a fiddle soars. But the two together—ah!

Who is he, Bob asks.

That's what I was wondering, says Charley.

Billy Gashade, boys, like I said. Billy Gashade. The Bride of Jesse James! His sweet Kansas City cousin. His darling, his Zee.

You don't say.

I'll be dog.

And who is *she* then.

She?

That one there. That Glory.

Oh. She ain't in the play.

Charley's expression, she notices, changes ever so slightly. Maybe he is trying to smile. Maybe trying to keep from smiling. He looks at her, then stretches his legs and eyes his boots. When he speaks, it is as though he means only those boots to hear. A dancer, he says, she is a dancer. She ain't in the play.

They sit, they talk. How long, she is sure she can't say. A fly circles the spittoon, a branch rubs against the window pane. That warmth—is it her blood. Slow down, she wants to say, be still, let me be calm, let my skin rest a spell. There is no music in this room, no call to dance, these voices not hers, not Esther whispering, not Mary Elizabeth singing nor Alice sobbing over her embroidery. This is not desire, familiar and insistent though it be. It is her knowledge, the breath and the blood of it. Unspeakable. Banal and pure as death.

Father's hands. The dark hole of his mouth.

There's music in your soul.

Mother's footsteps on the stairs. Her breath, then the quick whisper of crinoline and silk.

Billy is quiet. Asleep, she would say, asleep with his eyes open, this room and these voices *his* dream. Sister, he says, Sister, I am not the man I seem, not the one you see. I was here, but am not now. The one you will remember, that one will be me, that will be your brother, your true Billy, your truer sister.

Hush, Billy. Foolish dreamer. What do you know.

Beauty. Sister, I know beauty. I become beauty.

What good is it, she wonders.

As good, he says, as gold. Better. The currency of the spirit. What we were paid for with.

I'm in debt. I'm mortgaged to the hilt. My cash is spent.

You haven't dug deep enough in your pocketbook, Sister. It ain't your money to spend.

Woe is Billy, his grief his joy, his sadness delight. His skin has no more to do with him than his hat. Less. His hat, he will say, he has chosen. She'll take skin, good for nothing though it be. Grave skin. Warm today, tomorrow decay. Oh, but that warmth!

We have been called, Bob Ford says, the Merchants of Death. That is a exaggeration. Show us the money we made.

Precious little, Charley says. I'd give it all for that woman sitting there.

Is that, she wonders, a compliment?

Mr. Ford, that is my sister. Her worth—

Boys, boys. Let's keep to the business at hand.

Why don't she say something. Why does she just sit there like that. Who is she. I want to know who she thinks she is, sitting there saying nothing.

I regret my brother's behavior, Mr. Bunnell. He ain't hisself.

Charley, shut up. We got business to attend to.

She is my business.

Just now, Charley, our business is Jesse James. I want to understand some things, and I need your help.

Mr. Bunnell is right, Charley.

He was not my friend. I never knew him as a friend.

In Nashville he was known as Charles Havard, in Kansas City as T. J. Jackson. In Saint Joe, it was Thomas Howard.

He called his Colt *Baby*, his Smith & Wesson *Beauty*.

Often he spoke of Quantrill, his dead Captain.

To his son he sang:

> *Up, comrades, up, the moon's in the West,*
> *And we must be gone ere the dawn of day.*
> *The hounds of old Penick will find out our nest*
> *But the Quantrill they seek shall be far, far away!*

To his daughter he said, Look to your dear mother. She'll never lead you astray.

They remain seated the whole time, in a circle, Billy to her right and Bunnell to her left, across from her Charley Ford and his brother Bob. No one has moved for the longest time. Bob jerks his head to one side and spits. Charley stares at her, then at his boots. The boots, she notices, are new. They have high heels. She can smell the leather. Bunnell seeks certain facts, his voice like a wheel, now squealing, now scraping. Billy breathes deep, sighs, buttons his coat, unbuttons it, clears his throat, hums beneath his breath *Jesse James, Jesse James*, now and then says, Yes. Very true. As I thought. As I knew.

Later, with Charley Ford in a rented room, she remarks the mystery, as if it were what they sat around and were surrounded by.

Charley, what do you make of it.

Jesse James is dead, he says, killed by my brother Bob.

Did you know him well?

As well as I wanted to, as well as anybody. He was not my friend.

Did you want him dead?

I don't want to talk about that. Give me time.

Smiling, you look just like Bob.

I'm Charley, good as dead.

All that talk. Makes me wish I'd known Jesse James.

You'd regret it. He'd make you sorry. That was his way.

All the same she wonders, Charley beginning his slow caress, about Jesse James, what manner of man was he, how he might watch her, touch her, that bank robber, his hand in hers, his blood drumming, his voice soft like her daddy's, Billy's sad beauty. She can hear him now, Jesse James. I'm not beautiful, he says. I'm not even true. A bandit, I wanted too much. Everything, everything.

Then he pauses. He takes back his hand and she sees he has a finger missing.

Glory, Jesse says, I'm going to tell you the truth:

> *I know your daddy. I made him give you that dulcimer.*
> *I know your brother. I'm the fiddler he hears.*
> *On her deathbed your mother knew me.*
> *I have stole the hearts of your sisters.*

Here he winks at her.

> *Charley Ford is about to befriend me.*

She hears that clear as day, and when Charley, in the throes of his passion, calls out Glory Hallelujah she believes she's heard right and begins, in earnest, to return his embrace, touch for touch.

THE TRAGEDY OF BOB FORD

Bob Ford, the slayer of Jesse James, went out to Colorado, thought he would start himself a new life. How could he have known any better? Though his mama still cared for him, loving him from on high, he reckoned he was pretty much alone in this world, brother Charley having shot himself through the head, and there wasn't no woman to speak of, a trail of whores that started and ended in Kansas City, leading him in circles, dazed and crazy for love, through Saint Louis, Chicago, Pittsburgh, N.Y.C., and others too numerous to mention, including Boston and Philadelphia. These women all had took advantage of him. They saw him as a famous and wealthy man, and lay in wait for him at the doors of the opera houses, all smiles, eyes bright, lifting the hems of their skirts so that he might better imagine the woman under the silk. Turn away, Bob, he tells himself. Look not on that slim shank, gaze no more on that dainty foot in its smooth boot. No, sir. Keep your eye on your pocketbook, son. Might as well talk to a stump, off he goes, a fool and his money, up the stairs, down the hall, into the sweet-smelling room, his doom and damnation. But bless him if he can keep from believing otherwise, she so fine, it never fails, and he so mean, sure as the devil. A brief belief it is, and then the cursed knowledge, the blamed insight clear as day, as though with the money goes the soul, a chunk of it at a time, and him left holding the bag, the husk of hisself, skin deep.

In Colorado, he has heard, a fellow can do as he damn well

pleases. It is wide open country where you can get in on the ground floor. Mr. Bunnell, he says, I believe I will go out West. I begin to tire of these melodrammers.

Bob, says Bunnell, I will respect your wishes in this matter. But think it over. Do not make a hasty decision you will later regret. Does the money not suit you? Is the cash not to your liking, son? No one gets a higher percentage of the take. I am afraid I can do no better in that regard, if that is what you're hankering for.

No, sir. It is not the money.

Well, what is it then? Tell me and I will see what I can do.

But there's no telling Bunnell nothing. Bunnell has done all he can do, and soon will begin telling him so, reminding him how Bob Ford was nothing, the lowest of the low, when George Bunnell took him and his poor demented brother Charley and put them upon the boards in the limelight, them that never set foot on a theatrical stage before, giving them a honest way to make a buck off of the public's sincere desire to see the men that done in Jesse James. All they had to do was play theirselves. And if the booing and the heckling bothered their poor sensitive souls, why, they might have a laugh on the hecklers when the take was divided, mightn't they not?

The truth was—hell, who knows.

He thinks a lot about Charley, though he tries not to. He thinks a change in scenery will do him some good.

The truth is, Bob, says Bunnell, I think this thing may be about played out anyways. Folks are not as interested in Jesse James as they was when we first started out. When I first took the part of the Bandit King, and strode onto the boards, pistols drawn, you could hear the hush, whether we was playing Baltimore or Boston. Now—well, I just don't know. It is not the same. The public, I'm

Martha stands before the big stove, stirring the beans.

Where's that little girl, he asks. Where's my sweet Aurora Lee.

She's no little girl, Brother. And I don't know where she is. She has got a mind of her own, just like her daddy. She will run herself to the ground and die doing what pleases her, the spitting image of her daddy.

A good dose of her mama too, he'd say, but he refrains from pointing this out. Why rile her any more than she already is. He believes she was born riled, and there hasn't ever been any calming her, but you can work at it and keep her pretty much at her natural level.

Dick's here I see.

Yes.

Been here long?

Long enough.

You marry him?

He is trodding dangerous ground, he knows, pursuing this line of questioning. Sometimes he forgets himself. But he won't find out nothing at all without asking a few questions. She's never been one to volunteer information. One time he comes back and asks about his mama's health. Been dead a year, Martha says.

She puts the lid on the beans and turns around.

I never ast him to marry me, she says.

It surprises him how old she looks, how much when she moves she looks like his mama, the way she holds her head up like she was looking for cobwebs high up on the walls, her jaw firm, her hands pressed palms flat against her broad thighs. Once was enough, she says. I like it fine being a widow. It is better than being a wife, it has all the advantages and none of the disadvantages. You might as well sit down. You ain't leaving yet, are you.

I mean to stay a day or two. I'll sit, thank you.

She walks to the door, looks back through the house.

All he does, she says, polish them pistols, shine them boots.

You want, I'll have a talk with him.

I know how you talk, Brother.

Sister, I am a changed man from what I once was. You would not know me in a crowd. I am not so ornery as I use to be.

You sound like Charley. That is just how Charley talked when he showed up here so sudden. Then he shot his brains out.

You don't have to tell me about Charley. I know all I want to about Charley.

Maybe you need to know more, Brother.

He was not a success on the boards. I had to whisper his lines to him. I had to watch him all the time when we was backstage. He was likely as not to stroll onto the stage, plop himself down in the midst of a scene he was not suppose to be in. It was Charley that brought the boos and the jeers that closed us down in Buffalo and in Providence. It was hard to be patient with him. Now *I* want to play Jesse James, he told Mr. Bunnell. You be Charley for a change.

When he came here, he said, Sister, I am crazy for love. I love everybody and everything. I love the toad and the lily, the lake and the tree that stands beside the lake, I love the light coming down soft as hair. I forgive the crows.

To me he said, It is all meanness, nastiness and spite is all there is. Looks at me with them spaniel eyes so mournful and full up to the brim with tears. Charley, I told him, Charley, I said, you got to get a grip on yourself. I am holding as hard as I can hold, he says, but I am slippery, I'm greasy. That was when I felt a chill. I told him to say no more. I felt as though I was him. I might go, I realized, at any moment, blood booming and skin burning, my own body, my sweet head and beloved feet alike, burn away and leave this cold post that is at the center of me standing like a memorial amongst the trees. Do you hear what I am saying, Sister. It is not easy to say what has to be said.

Brother, towards the end Charley said, Glory Hallelujah. It was about all he would say. His eyes shining but getting tinier, deeper in his head, his thin lips opening, preparing to say them two words, sometimes sounding as though asking a question, sometimes as though giving advice. Ask him what is the matter, what does he want, and it is Glory Hallelujah. I keep Aurora Lee away from him. In the mornings he likes to sit in the corner where the sunlight might slant across his chest, the cat curl up on his lap, purring like the dickens while he runs his hand over her fur. Once I saw him lean down and whisper something to the cat. I believe he said, Jesse James, you are Jesse James, I know you are Jesse James. Seeing me, he stopped. Glory Hallelujah, he says, and the cat jumps down, is out of the room in a jiffy. Charley doesn't move. He says nothing more. I knew then that the end was near. I knew I might die any time. So I went after Dick Liddil and got him to love me. We was in the barn when we heard the shot. The poor bastard, says Dick, but I felt no pity. I was frightened. Brother, I have never been so afraid. Hold me, Dick, I said, but it wasn't no use. We found him in the cornfield, his face down in the dirt. Lord help us, I said to Dick. It wasn't pity I felt, just fright, pure lowdown fright.

It ain't nothing to be ashamed of. I have felt it many a time.

I still feel it. Right now I feel it.

I do too. I'm scared to death.

Ain't it awful.

I wisht I had the words, Sister, to describe it.

Aurora Lee has grown up tall, she is almost as tall as he is, and in plenty of other ways she is no little girl but a regular flesh and blood woman that any man might grow fond of. He sees some of Martha in her eyes, a look that seems to say I may be tired, honey, but do not count me out, and her hands flash about like barn swallows, swift and small and white, that know where they are going without her having to tell them. Uncle, she says, take me with you to the silver mines. You will see what a help I can be.

You ain't going nowhere, says Dick. You are staying here and helping your mama. Pass me them grits.

With *you* gone, she won't need no help. You're what makes all the work around here.

Hush, says Martha, but Dick, even with a mouth full of grits, grins at that one, and Martha looks at her plate as though she has lost sight of the food.

Don't I adequately repay you ladies, says Dick. Are you not satisfied with the service I provide.

Dick pushes his food into neat, distinct portions on his plate, squaring off the edges and eating one section at a time. It looks, Bob thinks, as if he is eating a map.

When I'm gone, maybe you'll appreciate me more.

I'd like to see you work a mine, Dick Liddil.

Maybe I won't. Maybe me and Bob has got other plans. Maybe we'll get the boys together again.

Lord, I'm so tired of this place, says Aurora Lee. Why can't I come along with you. I go into town, I work for Mrs. Willard one day, Mrs. Conway the next. Some days I think I cannot possibly flatten another shirt, shine another spoon. George Conway says I deserve better. I think he is surely correct. Uncle Charley would have understood. Uncle Charley use to hold me on his lap and say, Baby, don't let them suck you under.

In Colorado there's nothing for a young lady like you.

There's mountains. I know there's mountains.

You'd fall in a hole. Then where'd you be.

I'd walk and walk until I came to the center of the mountain.

Then what?

Maybe I'd go deeper.

My Lord, Bob thinks, she sounds just like poor Charley.

That's enough of that kind of talk, Martha says. Leave us eat our supper in peace.

George Conway says I'm beautiful as a angel. I might up and fly away any minute, he says, and he wouldn't be the least bit surprised.

It has been a while, Bob says, since I have had grits, Martha. In the North they don't know the delicacy.

You don't say.

Beauty like that should not go unrewarded. That's what George Conway says.

Daughter, did he offer you the cash?

Beauty is all around us, George says. It is in the very air we breathe.

You ain't so special then, are you.

Folks, we pay for that air. Every breath of it we breathe we pay for.

Bob's right. I'm broke paying for it.

George says I'm what makes him pay attention to the beauty that is everywhere abounding. I am filled with light, he says.

What he means is he can see right through you, honey.

I like it when George talks to me that way. Most men act like their tongues was made of stone. I like a man that can say what he feels.

You pay for that too. What you feel, you pay for.

Maybe then, says Martha, you shouldn't feel nothing.

And stop breathing while you're at it, Dick says.

I wisht I liked George better. He talks sweet, but has such ugly teeth. They are rotting away. When he talks, they move, they wobble, they lean this way and that.

It's always something.

I reckon it'll be over shortly.

That's the truth.

Amen, Sister.

Such tall trees. And the sun, why, surely that is not the same sun! It is bigger, to give such warmth, to make such colors with such flimsy clouds, it must be bigger, it must be what keeps the tops of the mountains smooth, more heat the higher you go. This is not Colorado, no. Colorado can wait, it will come in its own time. He has come as far as he needs to for the time being. Let's make us a sign, Dick. Let's see what we can do in New Mexico.

Don't we first got to get us a building.

There it is. Cast your eyes thataway.

I don't see a thing. I don't see nothing that suits. It's all back behind us.

Hell you say. We'll build the building we need. Right here. I see it in my mind's eye. It is white. It is between them two pines. The peaks of the mountains look like they come out of the roof. The branches of the pines brush against the window panes.

You don't say.

Sure as I live and breathe.

How could he have known that the spot was over a pit, that they would end up here in this storefront that smells, even after Dick has scrubbed and whitewashed the walls, like a corncrib. Once we get the whisky in circulation, he tells Dick, it will be different, you will see. But no. Every morning it is the same. Like a corncrib. It is downright saddening. People ain't going to come here, Dick says. It ain't lively enough. There's no whores. The walls smell like sin. They will come, says Bob. You will see. But he begins to lose heart. He watches the men saunter in, their eyes giving them away, fear breaking loose in the whites of their eyes like veins that soon will connect one end of the globe to the other.

He has noticed that Dick has begun to neglect his boots.

I thought we was going to Colorado.

We'll get there. We'll head up there soon's we get the money.

At night Charley walks up to him, his eyes like deep pools, shimmery and clear. You and me and Martha, he says, we got to get across. Across what, Charley. Already Charley's gone. It's dark, and the air is in short supply, like in the mountains. You have to breathe in more than you breathe out. He's running through the trees towards a cave. In the cave Jesse lies on a cot, his bare feet sticking over the edge, such small white feet, the toes lined up like little candles. Beside Jesse, in a rocking chair, sits Charley, stroking Jesse's forehead. This is the place, he says, that the bullet entered. Charley points to his own eye, a hole now, big enough to step into. Back there Martha stands among the corn stalks, the sky behind her hung with strips of silk, a closet of some kind that he might hide in if only it was possible to get there. I'm not letting you, Charley says.

In the morning he rides up into the hills. Below, the valley looks like an ear, the town a few specks, freckles, on the lobe. To the north rise up the mountains—the beginning of the Sangre de Cristo range—gray peaks soft against a rosy haze, lovely and calm, common as spit, strange all the same. *I'd walk and walk until I came to the center of the mountain. Then I'd go deeper.* Won't find nothing. Beauty? Hell. A hard place. Poor Charley'll tell you. Follow the Sangre de Cristos and you will get to where Jesse James never was. You will be in Colorado. Silverton, Telluride, Climax,

Stumptown. Creede and Liberty and Royal Flush. Jimtown and Pearl. The names of the towns hum in the pine needles, nothing but cold wind, dreams of silver.

All day he rides the ridges, follows the streams deep into the gorges, the pines dancing in the wind and the wind stinging his cheeks. He knows something is following him, a posse that ain't going to let up. Strong men mounted on strong horses. A posse of fathers. They see him but they wait. Plenty of time. They have been after him all his life and they will keep coming, sweat shiny on the horses' haunches, no matter how fast he rides, how slyly hide, his own daddy in the lead, tall and gaunt and erect in the saddle.

All right, Dick, It has come to this. We will act the melodrammer.

This is how it is. Maybe he will get to Colorado and maybe he won't. Maybe it don't matter where he gets to. In the silver camps of Colorado the men will ride in from their claims on the backs of stout jackasses, shoulders slumped, saddlebags empty, shovel and pick rattling like chains sure enough. Deeper tomorrow, they say. Farther up. Over along the ridge. You can see it agleaming in the sun, yellow ore and white. Put your nose to the dirt. It has a smell like nothing else, clean and rare and strong—listen—it is taking a deep breath as it makes its way towards the buried glittery heart of the mountain.

Men of New Mexico! I beg your indulgence, I ask your attention. I am the man that slayed Jesse James. His time was come, his race was won. I, the one that dispatched him to his Lord's reward. I took aim, I fired the ball that found the hidden outlaw's heart. What manner of man was he that fell? It is natural curiosity makes you want to know. To satisfy yourself, and to entertain and educate yourself in the bargain, come to tonight's performance of The Tragedy of Jesse James. This is guaranteed no ordinary melodrammer. This is from real life, acted by them that lived in those times and did the deeds. It is history before your very eyes.

He steps down from the chair, carries it back inside, sits on it. Now what, says Dick, handing him a glass of whisky.

We wait for the crowd. We call in the fiddler. Then we act the Tragedy.

I may forget. My memory's not much count.

It will come back.

I'm not accustomed to remembering.

Once you begin, I'm telling you, there's no stopping.

My memory plays tricks on me sometimes.

It's all tricks.

Well, then—

Just keep to the story. Start at the beginning. Go to the end.

Seems like a long ways.

We got all evening. And the next.

And the next.

That's the idea.

I feel a little sick. I'm ill, Bob. The trip's greatly weakened me.

I'll shoot you early. Then you can rest. You'll make a dandy Jesse James.

It's easier for you. You play yourself.

It's nothing that's easy.

I never cared for Jesse James.

He wasn't so bad, Dick. He had his virtuous points.

Name one.

He loved his mama.

He was mean. He was spiteful. A man of malice. Dick, he said to me, Dick, he said, you ain't worth shit.

What he did, he did well.

I saw him shoot a dog once.

He was loyal to his brother.
And you the one that killed him!
Yes, and it is our salvation, right?
Some salvation.
It's all we got.
Why, save ourselves, I reckon it is.
You reckon right.
What have we come to.
Not much. As much as anyone.
The hell you say.
The hell I say.
Is it time?
Open the doors. Tell that fiddler start the overture.

ZERELDA JAMES SAMUEL

It's one long leave-taking hard on the heels of another. Robert, she says, must you go, must you leave me, leave your strapping young sons, your baby daughter, leave this your family in the prime of your life and for what, the promise of gold, a dream of money. For God's sake, remember me and write to me. She remembers that handsome man, that preaching man, that blue-eyed man, fine of feature, slight of build, his dark coat too big for him though made to fit, as though he is always sloughing skin, secretly, just a little every day, sneaking back to soul. Gone for gold, then for good, no gold, not an ounce ever sent back to her who waits in Missouri with them three growing and ever-hungry children and the memory of a revival-crazed husband, a Baptist to boot.

Goodbye, Robert James. Goodbye.

Goodbye, Frank. Susan. Jesse. My Dr. Reuben Samuel. The earth itself passes away, don't it. Watching it, you can imagine that just out there beyond the windowglass, beyond that stand of windblown elms and stretching from there to the horizon, is Frank's land, his farm he calls it when it is plain as day that no crop worth the name will rise from that hard red dirt and he'd best settle for cattle and be done with it. It is land, he says, it is my land. Yes, but it will pass away, even as just now it passes with the speeding of this train across Oklahoma. It will be blown out from under you, you wait and see. She watches the trees. Not many. Not enough to shield nothing. *Goodbye*. Missouri will be along soon enough. Can't be any too soon.

But, my, this Oklahoma is a long state to get across. Indian Territory it used to be, all this land the land of the savages. Don't see so many Indians out there, unless they live in farmhouses now, with windmills and picket fences. Life goes on, things change. Don't they though. Zerelda, Robert says, a man has got to take advantage of the opportunities that present themselves. He's not smiling, and he holds her hand clasped in both of his so firm she thinks he might mean harm to it. It's the hand she has no more, the one gone with half the arm when the Pinkertons, them bastards, them sons of bitches, throw their bomb through the window of the house and kill her Archie, her dear little son by Dr. Reuben Samuel, thinking to get her other sons of course, the ones by Robert. Gone or not, she still feels Robert's grip on that hand, the rough edges of his palm pressing, his fingers stiff as sticks. I'll send for you, he says, I'll write soon as I get there. I'll be missing you. I'll be loving you in my heart.

And panning gold with his hands until his heart thumps its last. Dead not two weeks after getting there, and so when she thinks *gone to California* she thinks it's goodbye for good, a chase for the grave, California just another word for purgatory, a long wait in the farthest West once you get there. Maybe he'll send for her yet. In the meantime—which is to say this life—she means to keep herself on the move.

Across the aisle from her sit a gentleman and a lady. They look straight ahead, as though Oklahoma's passing beyond their window means nothing to them. The lady, her tiny feet in pumps that look narrow as corn cobs, her hands gloved tight in gray suede, looks across the aisle at her from time to time, just a quick glance. Can't catch her at it. Can't meet her eyes. The man you can't even catch breathing. Stiff! She's seen St. Joe store dummies show more signs of life.

There is a resemblance though. In the woman she sees a resemblance to her Susan. Lord, what if Susan had married such a man as that one. Some things you can be grateful for. Parmer's a man, at least, a rancher, a Texan, a big handsome man with hands thick like her Robert's, no preacher's hands, and feet that move beneath him as though they are in charge, they are deciding where to carry him to next.

Woman, she says, you look like my daughter.

Nudges her, reaches across the aisle with her whole arm, leaning outward so as to leave no question who's being spoke to. You, girl. It's you I'm talking to. That's right. A body's got to make conversation, pass the time. I am one of them that needs conversation. I do not seek out solitude.

The woman smiles, her man clearing his throat, patting—she can see this good enough all right—his knee with the tips of his long fingers. So he is alive. But can he speak.

That is a handsome ring, she says to him. I like to see a man wear a ring. My son was in the habit of wearing two.

The man clinches his fist, then opens it quick, like he hasn't meant to do that, he has nothing to hide. Out the window there's not a tree in sight. Grazing land, the grass beaten down, almost white this time of year, the sky closed off, one unbroken cloud, smooth as horseflesh, not a speck of sunlight coming through, she don't know where the light's coming from.

Do you have the time of day, she asks, and there's Frank, how he does show up at the unlikeliest times, that boy, looking like he wants bad to smile but can't, don't know how, his hands narrowing, not the better to see her, no, but as if to block out as much of her as possible. He'd not look at anything, she believes, if it meant he'd be safe from the world, hid inside himself. Well, Frank. What is it this time.

Not a speck of sunlight coming through, but all this brightness.

Mother, Frank says. I'm leaving Missouri. This country's no place for me.

Is he going to California then? No, he goes to Tennessee, does Frank, his brother with him, their wives, their children. There's no stopping them. When they come back, she will tell them, Stay, it is enough, but she might as well say, Lord, give me back my arm, you have had it long enough.

If you are wondering about my arm, she says to the lady and gentleman, I would be glad to tell you the story, though it's not very pleasant. In fact it is downright grim. It is what my boy Frank would call a tragedy.

Jesse has been her favorite. Why not say it, it's Jesse with his blue eyes like her Robert's, his smile like her daddy's, a wisp of a smile but it's there, he's the one pleases her most, neglect her though he will and Frank profess his endless devotion, his vow to take care of her until she take her final leave. Gone is Jesse, gone like her Robert to the grave, chased there, poor boy, by them that would profit from an orphan's tears, a widow's wail, bankers and their henchmen, those robbers in dapper waistcoats and spit-shiny oxford shoes.

The man looks at his lady—she knows that look all right—and the two of them rise without so much as a pardon-me and walk, heads high and still as alert hens, both of them like hens, walk to the front of the car and reseat theirself, the lady hen this time taking the seat by the window—so that the gentleman hen can protect her no doubt, pretend to be a rooster. Goodbye then. Goodbye and good riddance.

She waves her stump of an arm at them. Hens.

Ticket, ma'am?

He smells of shoe polish, but his boots are dull, worn. Perhaps it is the uniform, blue like the federals wear when they come to do their mischief. Uniforms smell like shoe polish and feel like wood just varnished, too smooth for anything cloth. Frank, in his rebel gray, hugs her—Farewell, Mama!—and it is like being in the clutches of a tree, the bark of it stripped off. Let go of me, boy. Let go and go do what you got to do.

Yes, she has her ticket. Used to be there was no need for it. She boards a train and is recognized, she is *their* mother, the lost arm her ticket to wherever she wants to go. Step right up, Mrs. Samuel. Find you a good seat. She'd like a seat by the window, thank you. And a companion who knows how to listen. She does not want—she smiles, they always laugh at this—her other arm talked off, thank you. Oh, Mrs. Samuel, how you do go on.

How indeed. On and on.

Now they don't know who she is. It is Nineteen-hundred and eleven, for nearly six weeks it has been 1911, and no one remembers who she is. My, sometimes, she forgets herself. Someone will have to poke her, she imagines, when her name is called and it is time to take her leave. Yes, she has her ticket. Good all the way to Kansas City.

For some must watch while some must sleep.... He's full of quotations, is Frank. She watches him read, his little eyes, bless them, wide as they ever do get, his thin lips moving as little as possible. It should have been better for him, it should have been better for all of us. What good has his Shakespeare done him. Robert's gold, no better than his Bible. Oh, she'll not mock that book. No. God has His reasons, no doubt. A waste of time to try to figure them out. *Thus runs the world away.*

Tell me this, she asks. Just where is it that we are all going, when we are going away from each other. That's what I'd like to know. Tell me that.

But there's no one there. She has forgotten. She sees them up there in front of her and on the other side of the aisle, the backs of their heads letting the dark through, holes in the light. There's no one else in the car and not a station to stop at and pick up more before Oklahoma City. Just now Oklahoma City seems a long ways. The landscape outside the train window is barren. It seems not to move, all the trees gone. She may die before reaching Oklahoma City. Then where'll she be. Where her arm's at, she hopes. Whole again, wherever. Or else all empty, everything gone. What use is it, though, to go away and leave your flesh behind. She's grown fond of it. It's not the flesh it once was, no, not the soft skin Robert touches—seldom enough, to be sure, but when he does, well, there's never been another like that lanky, loose-boned, big-handed preacher—no, it's not that skin but it's her skin, she has no other.

She hears something. Is it singing. Somebody singing. Comes from the gentleman and the lady, but their mouths ain't moving, unless her seeing's gone bad. She searches the depths of her bag for her glasses—there they are, already on her face, Well, then, she must move closer. Does, and they're the same distance, singing the cheerfulest hymn she's ever heard and their lips not moving at all. How do they do that. She means to get in close enough to touch their lips, to make out the words.

Impossible. Something has hold of her legs. If she stands she will fall. Let go, damn you. Why're you holding me back. Ain't I lady enough. Ain't I good enough.

Her father comes to her and says, Zerelda, you must never disobey your mother. You must always respect her, no matter how unreasonable she may seem to you. She is a good woman. At heart she is a good woman. Runs off with another man. A good woman, her father says.

His eyes not looking at her—she remembers that—and how

his hands lay on his thighs like they was not hands at all, the longer she looks at them the stranger they become, hunks of wood, rock slabs, broke china. He has taken her to mass, miles away, such a long ride in the flat and hard bed of the wagon, over rough and dusty roads, in order that the priest the father may hear her confess. A dark room smelling of potato sacks shelved in the root cellar, but you are not alone, even when finally he absolves you and you can go. The Lord always with you. Watching. Peeking. That Holy Ghost.

Idolatry, says Robert, such a soft voice and him a preacher, his young skin smooth, more like her mother's than her father's, the fingertips blunt but delicate as little leaves afluttering across the surface of your flesh, just so, there, touching the nape of your neck. You was raised up, he says, in a idolatrous religion. Yes, she says. Oh, yes. Wishing he might never stop telling her. She will go anywhere with him. Please tell her what she must believe. *Save me.*

From what. From nineteen hundred and eleven. This train, Robert. You know I'm here, don't you, not a idolatrous thought to my name, a convent girl unconfessed these, what is it, these sixty, no it is seventy years. That has lasted, damn you, sins as fleeting in the commission as in the regretting.

This is dying, that's what this is. That is why she can't move, why the trees have disappeared, why beyond the window Oklahoma has stopped running away. Mary, Mother of God, has hold of her ankles. Quit now. She kicks but Mary hangs on, her grip like a fact of life, no more than that. Enough, enough.

How far, she calls to the couple, is Oklahoma City.

Singing, they don't hear nothing.

Oh, they sing all right. They keep to theirselves their secrets, their blood beating beneath their skin, shooting for the heart and hitting, in secret, keeping time hid in a dark place inside. Everybody the same. She's not going to blame them. Nobody's to blame.

She rises. Come along, Mary. It is as though the train has stopped in order to free her from her place, permit her to walk up the aisle to where the gentleman and the lady sit. Nothing's holding her back. She's been imagining things, sitting there like a child, letting her fancies get ahold of her. She is eighty-five years old or is it eighty-six, a grown woman surely, with a mind of her own. She intends to live to a hundred. She means to do what she pleases. It is the privilege of age, this liberty. Look at this arm I've lost.

Well, she says, here I am. Move away from me and I follow. Let's talk. Stop that singing now and talk to me.

She has never seen the likes of this. Singing and their mouths closed. Pretending they don't hear her, don't see her. In the convent the biggest one, the one with cheeks rimmed like squash, says Jesus is going to whip whoever is a bad girl, he can see everybody all the time. She's glad that she's good, has her catechism by heart. It must be Jesus, seeing her now and remembering, who gives her the strength to rise and walk away from the grip of Mary. Jesus or Robert. She is grateful, whoever, though if it is Robert he must understand that she don't intend to let him off the hook so easy. He has got some explaining to do, going away and leaving her with three children, a farm best fit for weeds, and a promise of gold. In her dreams he stands at the doorway, says, Zerelda, love of my life, why don't you come along with me, then hides so that she can't tell where he's at, not even if she looks behind every bush, every rock, in every cave. Catch a glimpse of him, see his shadow, his face bright as a lamp, but up close it's just her father. Why're you so late, he says. Zerelda, what trouble have you gotten into.

Mortal trouble. Awake, she knows it's mortal, but of course he's gone and she reckons can't hear her. Won't ever forgive her anyway. You are leaving the Church, he says, those strange woodlike hands laying there in his lap like they was nailed down, glued, varnished and polished smooth. You are leaving the Church for a Baptist preacher. You are putting your soul in dire peril.

I married Robert James, she tells them, when I was seventeen years old. My convent education never took. I became a Baptist and raised my children Baptists. I bore him three children. Then he went away. Then they went away.

I know who you are. You are my Jesse. I recognize you.

Everything he done, he done because he had to, because men drove him to it. Always he had to take his leave before he was ready to.

They was raised up right, all my children. Raised by the Good Book. Mama, Jesse says, hear what I know by heart: For God so loved the world that He gave His only begotten Son, that whosoever believeth in Him shall not perish but have everlasting life. John 3:16. He had it by heart and never forgot.

Both of you boys always had strong memories.

They went off to look for their father's grave. They went all the way to California. They had to find it. It's no use, Reuben told them, but they had to go. It was after the war and there was no arguing with them. They were men sure enough and they were going to find their daddy's grave if it killed them. Jesse hugged me. He kissed me on the mouth and his lips were like porcelain, as cold and hard, and they both kneeled and held my hands, Frank the left, Jesse the right, the one gone now, and looked me long in the eye and swore always to love me and never to forget all I had done for them in the days of their youth.

I never forgot, Mama.

No, you never forgot. I know that, Frank.

Made her feel like a queen the way they kneeled down in front of her. Kissed her hands. My sons! Promise me you'll come back.

Outside the window the trees are little as bushes. No groves. They grow alone, squat close to the ground. You'd have to crawl under them for shade. I like this country, Frank says. I like to see all around me. I like my creeks narrow and my ravines shallow. I like the flat land, the big sky, the roads leading straight to where you want to go. I like the thunderheads, I like most everything but the wind and the sleety winters.

What they need to understand is that she never insists on his coming back. No, she remembers being surprised to hear it. I'm coming home, Mama, he writes, like I promised. I'm coming back to Missouri. This country don't suit me. Will any country ever suit him, her blue-eyed Jesse.

I missed you, Mama. It was like a part of me was gone.

Don't talk to her about parts being gone.

So he's got to move back to Missouri, everybody on the hunt for him, you can't trust nobody, at least there's kin in Missouri. Him with his young wife, his cousin that was named after her, Zerelda Mims from Kansas City, her sister's girl, and them children that remind her so much of her own that she can hardly stand it, the girl honey-eyed and rosy-cheeked just like Jesse, climbing onto her lap and saying, Nanna, how come your arm's not all there.

It's there. You just can't see it.

Or: I once had another son. He was named Archie. When he died he took that arm with him. He didn't want to go, you see, but if he had to he wanted me to come with him. He was just a little fellow. Archie, I said, that wouldn't be fair to my other children. They are grown, but they need me too.

That's right, Mama.

Well, says Archie, if you won't come with me at least let me have your arm always around my shoulders to keep me warm.

He's her baby and she can't refuse him. Do you blame her? She'll be leaving this world soon enough, and she reckons she'll be whole in the next world, wherever that may be.

The next stop is Oklahoma City.

That singing. Is it the hawks. It is the way hawks would sing, seems to her, not humans. A hymn sung by a hawk. Fancy that. Of course you couldn't make out the words. This is a country fit for hawks, plenty of sky. A crow perches on the shoulder of the gentleman, but she's through trying to tell him anything.

I been wronged, says the crow.

It faces her, its eyes, she swears, no crow's eyes at all, blue eyes, Jesse's eyes. So this is what it comes to. She remembers the wound, mortal sure enough, open and soft in the back of his head like lips, a better pair to replace the others that would never open to say what needed saying. She leans down to listen. *Caw, caw.* Is this a joke he's playing on her. Oh, this is some life, ain't it. When she was a girl, everything was forever, everyone together, her father's hands seldom moving, fixed on his lap or to the ploughshare, save when in the church at Lexington making the sign of the cross, and her mother always returns to the room, her basket filled with corn ears and muskmelons. Three sisters sleep in the trundle bed, the boys on pallets spread across the plank floor. At night the house itself seems to breathe, all around her breath in and out of the chinks, a sweet panting and now and then a sigh. *We are all together in this house.* But where are we now, nearing Oklahoma City, our souls in peril. How can she have known, the warmth of her sisters' young bodies aflowing in the trundle bed, they will all go away, not a one of them stay put there where they belong, she herself quick as any to depart, go off damned by her own father for the love of a sweet-talking Baptist with clear blue eyes and not a speck of dirt in his fingernails, big hands pale as a girl's, hair smooth like feathers. He holds her hand, the one that's gone now but she can still feel that touch, and she thinks, This is what I am meant for. Nothing's the same after that. *Goodbye, Father.*

She likes her chair by the window so that she may watch the progress of the trees. One of the privileges of age is that you can sit down, you are not always expected to be doing something, you can sit still by the window as long as you want to. The disadvantage is the solitude. You can keep your solitude.

Frank takes her to the station. She sees how worn down he is. He ain't as tall as he used to be. He is old, her little boy an old man, older than her own father, and his son is gone away, she thinks, to Texas.

Frank, do you know where your brother is.

Mother, Jesse's where we all're going.

No. He's right there on your shoulder. He's looking straight at me out of that crow's eyes.

That can't be.

I know my son's eyes. See how they are blinking.

I saw him lowered into the ground, Mother. You did too.

He must've went straight through, come out the other side.

But she remembers. She has him put in the yard so that she can watch out for grave-robbers. People come from all over the country, say, Mightn't we see where he's buried. For a small fee she lets them look. Sells pebbles from the site. When those pebbles run out, gets more from the creekbed. People coming all the time. Where is he. Beneath the ground you're standing on.

Take one of them little pieces of rock you want to, two bits each. It's nice to have a memento.

She remembers now.

Listen, she says to the couple, I am dying. I will be dead before this train can stop at Oklahoma City. You will have to carry me off. I am Zerelda Samuel, mother to Jesse James. Before I leave I want you to know how much I have appreciated your company these last hours of my life. If you would care for a keepsake, cut a swatch from the hem of my gown. It is good material and will last. Pass it on to your grandchildren. Tell them how you met me on this train in the middle of Oklahoma. Tell them I wish them the best. Tell them I said Goodbye. Tell them I said don't no one pity me, not when I am passed away.

Even though it be forever getting across Oklahoma, she means to say no more. She'll examine the scenery from now on. Not. much. All the same, it's what's there. That peculiar sky. Hawks and crows. No sun in sight, but light, light the whole way.

LIBRARY OF CONGRESS CATALOGING IN PUBLICATION DATA

Taylor, Robert, 1941 Oct. 19-
  Loving Belle Starr.

  1. Starr, Belle, 1848–1889—Fiction. 2. James,
Jesse, 1847–1882—Fiction. I. Title.
PS3570.A9518L6 1984 813'.54 83-25669
ISBN 0-912697-07-5